TURNING GRACE

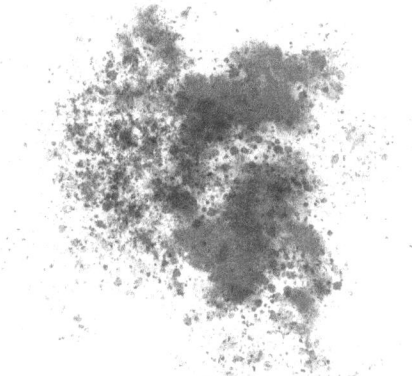

J. Q. DAVIS

Turning Grace
Copyright © 2014, 2019 by J.Q. Davis
All rights reserved.

Published: J.Q. Davis 2014, 2019
jq.davis@yahoo.com

Editing: Precy Larkins
Cover Design: Murphy Rae, Indie Solutions by Murphy Rae,
www.murphyrae.net
Formatting: Elaine York, Allusion Graphics, LLC,
www.allusiongraphics.com

TURNING
GRACE

To discovering who you truly are
and embracing it.

12 YEARS EARLIER...

I STILL COULDN'T BELIEVE this was all happening. My daughter didn't deserve this. She was so young. So innocent. She was just a child, and no child should ever be allowed to become this sick. I had no choice but to take her to the hospital. I wish I had known why this was happening to her. But it wasn't my specialty. Dr. Walker was smart. Smarter than me. I'd learned a lot from him in medical school. If I had to trust another doctor's opinion, it'd be Mark's.

"So, is she cured, Mark?" I asked Grace's doctor. I had known him for so long. I felt completely comfortable that he would be honest with me. Not that doctors were liars. I was a doctor. I never lied to my patients. But I knew Mark would be straightforward and professional. No sugarcoating.

"I believe she is. We didn't know what the outcome would be, but we did it. I believe she is cured. You know, children can be quite resilient when it comes to illness. It seems that she'll make a full recovery."

"Oh, thank goodness! Thank you so much for all that you have done."

"You are quite welcome. We'll be able to discharge her as soon as you and your husband sign off some paperwork. You know the drill."

My husband. I had not seen him for the past two weeks.

"Um...well, Jack is out of town at the moment. He won't make it back before we get home."

"Ahh. That's right. Well, Nurse Alex will get the discharge papers for you."

I couldn't wait to get my baby home. It had been such a long two weeks. How could this have happened to my little Gracie? I almost lost her. I did lose her. Now she was cured, and she needed to be home with her toys and her dog Lucy.

Oh, I just knew she missed her little puppy.

When I walked back into Gracie's hospital room, I fought back the tears. Her tiny body was lying motionless, asleep on a bed that looked ten sizes too big for her. The nurse had already pulled out what seemed to be a hundred different tubes from her body. It shouldn't have been anything new for me to see, but it was still heartbreaking. Seeing patients in similar situations was one thing, but when it was your little girl lying there, helpless, it was a different story.

The nurse handed me all the paperwork. She said, "Dr. Romero, should anything go wrong, just give us a call and bring her right back."

"Thank you so much, Alex. You have truly been a wonderful nurse to my Gracie." I swallowed back a few tears and squeezed her hand in mine before letting go.

"You're very welcome. Grace is a sweet little angel," Alex said, bandaging the last puncture hole on Gracie's arm.

I didn't want to have to wake her.

When everything was ready, I ran to get the car while the nurses helped Gracie to a wheelchair and met me downstairs. We secured her into the car seat, and she slept all the way home. I knew that she was still a bit groggy from all the medications she was given throughout the two-week stay. I just couldn't wait to get her home, in her comfortable bed and around all of her familiar surroundings.

Once I got her through the front door, I carried her to bed, tucked her in, and she fell right back to sleep a minute later. Lucy jumped into the bed with her and Gracie instantly wrapped her arms around the pup. I desperately wanted her to be herself again, running around in her normal manner. Bright-eyed, with her long curls dancing around her face. She was such a delight. She was so fun-loving and smiling all the time.

For the past two weeks, she had been so sick with fever and fatigue that I had forgotten how lovely her smile could be. I was confident that she would be herself again—it would just take some time.

I thought about making homemade soup for her while she slept. My grandmother made it, my mother made it, and my sister had just recently taught me how to make it. It was basically every vegetable you can think of, boiled in chicken broth and noodles. Every winter, my mother would make a large pot, and any sniffles or coughs were instantly remedied before we could even finish a bowl. It could quite possibly cure the common cold, if you asked me.

I was sure I had everything I needed. Carrots, potatoes, onions, spinach... I was never the best cook and Gracie was really hard to please. For being so young, she was a very picky eater. But I just stuck to the normal foods kids her age ate—chicken nuggets for dinner, Goldfish crackers for snacks. She was deathly afraid of vegetables, though. I often tried to hide it in her food, but she managed to figure it out. She had a long life ahead of her, and I knew that one day she would open up and try different things.

It was so quiet in the house. I was not used to this. Gracie was always playing with noisy toys and Jack would have the television blaring with a football game in the background.

Jack. I couldn't think about him at the moment. I had to concentrate on getting this soup made for my Gracie. I began prepping.

Ring-ring-ring!

Right as the phone rang, it startled me, and I nicked my index finger while cutting vegetables.

"Shit!" It didn't look too deep. I wrapped a paper towel around it and ran for the phone.

"Hello?"

"Hi! You're home. Good. I'm thinking of coming to see Gracie tomorrow. Is she doing okay?" It was my sister. She and I got along really well. She was a great aunt to Gracie, and Gracie adored her. When she received the devastating news that she could never bear children of her own, she became very close to her only niece.

"Hey. She's doing really well," I said. "You can come by tomorrow. I know she'll love that."

After about five minutes of leisurely conversation, we ended the call. My finger began to throb, but I paid no mind. I had to get this soup done before Gracie awoke.

When the soup was finished, I went to check on Gracie. She was still sound asleep. I fixed myself a bowl, watched a little TV, and realized I should get some sleep myself. I decided to sleep on the couch, just in case Gracie needed me in the middle of the night. Our living room was situated in the middle of the house, with Gracie's room on one side and the master bedroom on the other.

As I started to doze off, I could not help but think about Jack. Why hadn't he called? How could he just leave me with a sick child to go on a business trip? Normally, his business trips lasted about a week, sometimes a week and a half. But work always seemed more important. The last time we spoke on the phone, we fought. He said he would call me back. He never did.

Was he seeing someone else?

I'd guess I could be blamed as well. Our relationship was on the rocks. His job seemed more important and he never slowed down after Grace was born. Even though I had put my own career on hold to raise Grace, I should have appreciated the efforts he made to take care of us.

Just as my mind cleared and sleep set in, I was suddenly awakened by a sharp pain. I opened my eyes to complete darkness. The television must have been on a timer. Jack would oftentimes fall asleep out here, mostly during our frequent fights.

As I began to shift a little to get comfortable, pressure radiated from my hand, followed by an intense throbbing. I lifted it up to my face but could not see a thing. I sat up on the couch and leaned over to switch on the table lamp. When I turned back around, Gracie stood at the corner of the couch with blood smeared all over her mouth.

"Gracie!" I yelled. "Oh my God! Are you okay, sweetheart?" I grabbed her and began searching everywhere I could to find a wound or some kind of injury.

"Gracie! What is it? Where are you hurt?" I asked her frantically.

I could see in her eyes that she was completely frightened by my yelling. She stood still for a moment, then lifted her finger and pointed to the white quilt that covered my body. I looked down and nearly fainted when I saw that it was covered in blood. At that very moment, the pain seemed to have gone from about a five to a hundred and five.

I let go of her, and as I grabbed the quilt to pull it off, I noticed that my left hand was drenched in blood. It took a minute for my mind to focus on something other than the crimson red when finally, I realized that my index finger was no longer there.

THE DATE
Present Day

"GRACIE, HURRY UP! YOU'RE going to be late for school, dear!" I heard my mom yell from downstairs.

"I'm coming, Mom! Give me a minute!" I stared at myself in the bathroom mirror. What was up with the bags under my eyes? And my hair...

I briefly thought about dyeing it. My hair was easily my best feature. The long and curly brown locks hung below my shoulders. I have had people ask me if it was real. Why would I wear a wig? I was seventeen!

I felt like I needed a change. If only I could change the size of my boobs, too.

I turned to the side, revealing my small chest. I sucked in a breath of air and puffed my chest out, quickly releasing once I realized how ridiculous I looked.

"Honey!"

I took another long look and sighed. I knew that being a teenager was a time of change, but I just wished I could change much faster. I never used to be this crazy about my appearance. I'd guess the gorgeous senior girls at my high school weren't too reassuring for my self-confidence.

Realizing that there was nothing I could do about it and there was no sense in obsessing, I huffed out of the bathroom. I grabbed my bookbag and dashed down the stairs for breakfast.

"Finally," Mom murmured under her breath.

"Mom, why do I wake up every morning with these awful bags under my eyes?" I asked as I sat down at the table. I was so hungry.

"Let me see." She grabbed my chin and looked closely into my eyes. "Gracie, they're fine. Maybe you're just not getting enough sleep."

"I guess. But they end up going away later on in the day. It's been going on for a couple of weeks now. It's just weird. So, what's for breakfast? Please tell me it's cereal for a change." I pouted.

My mom was really big on having breakfast in the morning. She always said, since I could remember, that eating breakfast before your day starts is what gets your day started. I did agree with this theory, but her breakfast could feed a family of five! Scrambled eggs, toast, sausage links, bacon, ham, pigs-in-a-blanket, and a large glass of juice were the norm. I didn't think there was anyone else in the world who could eat that much for breakfast. But I always seemed to eat every last bit.

"Gracie, you know you need more than just cereal in the morning, dear. Remember, eating breakfast before your day starts—"

"Is what gets your day started," I finished, with a roll of my eyes.

"So, I have to be at the funeral home till late tonight. There's some paperwork I have to get done before I leave for the convention in Arizona on Halloween weekend. You can have leftovers tonight for dinner. Which reminds me, are you going to be okay while I'm gone? I have never left you alone before."

"Mom, I'll be fine. I'm seventeen years old. I think I can take care of myself now," I mumbled between bites of my pigs-in-a-blanket. "Besides, your absence is going to give me a chance to finally have that huge party I've been dying to have. You know. The one with all the drugs, sex, and alcohol. It's going to be great!" I cheered sarcastically.

"Gracie! That's not funny! Now finish your breakfast, or you'll be late. Oh, and don't forget your lunch. You're going to love what I packed today," she said with a glow in her eyes as she handed me my brown paper bag.

"Fine." I pouted again before I took a bite of my eggs.

The truth was that I worried about her having to work out of town. I had never been on my own. We didn't have many visitors come to the house. It was always just my mom and me. Dad left when I was a little girl, for reasons I was not completely sure of. Mom never really explained it to me, and whenever I'd ask, she would just change the subject.

I was an only child, and to be honest, I was okay with that. I had always kept to myself for the most part. I had friends—I was not some loser loner. But I liked that it was just me and my mom. We had a great relationship.

As I walked up the main staircase to the school's entrance, I remembered the first day of my freshman year. On that fateful day, there had been a dreadful thunderstorm. It ended right as I began my walk to school. But the main staircase steps were still wet, and I just so happened to slip and fall in front of the entire school.

Accidents happen, but when they do, does your skirt fly up over your head revealing the only clean pair of underwear you had that were, of course, granny panties with a huge hole in them? Well, that was what happened to me. And of course, it wouldn't be complete without a fresh new nickname to follow me throughout the entire course of my high school career.

Let's just say, I now always made sure my panties were new and holey-free.

"Hey, Granny-panty! Watch out for those stairs!"

And there it was. How three years had passed and anyone could still remember this was beyond me. But of course, Sonny Westwood never forgot a humiliating moment in someone else's life.

I glanced over my shoulder. There she was, surrounded by her perfect friends, wearing her perfect clothes, holding hands with the perfect guy who was running his fingers through her perfect, strawberry-blonde hair. Yes, she was the most popular of them all. And although it seemed so cliché and we have seen it in a million movies, she was very real at Middleton High. Everyone swooned over Sonny Westwood. Along with all of her perfect physical features and perfect fashion sense, Sonny had a very wealthy and perfect family, perfect grades, and all of the perfect accessories any perfect girl would need. But one of those perfect accessories should not have been in her possession, and his name was Tristen Miles.

"Sonny, come on. Are you ever gonna let that go?" I heard him ask as I walked by.

She giggled. "Well, that's her name!"

I turned my head and kept walking toward my locker.

Tristen Miles was tall, with just the right balance of muscular and slim tone to his body. Don't get me wrong, I liked The Rock's muscles, but I would prefer a guy who didn't seem like he could hug me and crush me into pieces. I found it really attractive when a guy was muscular, but you could only notice it when he moved his arm a certain way.

Tristen had longer, bed-head hair. Wavy and dark. I sort of had a thing for longer hair. I once saw a movie where Brad Pitt's hair was as pretty as mine. He lived on a farm and rode horses all day long, but it was hot. After seeing that movie, I couldn't help but imagine Tristen in a cowboy hat and boots.

He wasn't as preppy as the rest of the clique, though. It seemed that he dressed for comfort most of the time with jeans and a T-shirt. Close enough to a cowboy, I'd suppose.

He was a jock, of course. Played every sport Middleton had to offer. But swimming seemed to be his forte.

Speedos...now that was better.

He and Sonny began dating sophomore year, when he transferred here from Oregon. From what I knew, his mom and dad were doctors and he was an only child, like me. I believe we had some things in common, but I never really understood what common interests he had with Sonny. Apparently, they had been on and off for...well, ever since they started dating. She would dump him, date another guy, and then a week later end up with Tristen again. I couldn't comprehend why he would even put up with her. I mean, didn't she understand how amazing he—

"Grace, did you hear anything I just said?" someone said.

I came back down to Earth and my eyes finally focused on my best friend. I had no idea she was even standing in front of me. "Oh, sorry, Phoebe. Yes, I did."

No, I didn't.

"Are you fantasizing about him again? G, I don't think this is healthy. Your brain, like, completely goes into fart mode when you're within a thirty-foot radius of him. Seriously, I think you may need to just move on."

But I don't want to move on, the pouty voice in my head said.

She grabbed her books out of her locker, which was two doors down from mine.

"Look, he and Sonny are never going to end. It's so annoying with those two. Let's find you a boyfriend!" she shrieked, eyes widening at the thought of this.

She was right. I didn't ever have a chance. He thought I was a big joke, and he would never leave Sonny. It's been a vicious cycle for a long time. I hated it when Phoebe was right.

I shook the thoughts of Tristen for now.

"Okay, you're right. So, what were you saying?"

Phoebe continued to tell me about the sexy guy she worked with at the mall while we waited outside of homeroom for the bell to ring. I envied this about her. Phoebe Morgan was not wildly popular, but very social. She was definitely the social butterfly of the school. She made it a point to be friends with everyone—never hung out with just one group of people. You could catch her floating around during lunch hour, making her way through the variety of crowds scattered around the courtyard. The Preps, the Jocks, the Geeks, the Highs (the constantly stoned kids). We were the closest of friends, though. She lived a block down from my house, and we had been friends since we were in third grade. We went to elementary, middle, and now high school together.

Phoebe was the kind of girl that many other girls secretly envied and guys liked to hang out with, but I was the only really close girlfriend she had. I did secretly envy her, too, but I still thought highly of her. She was just so charismatic and really didn't care what anyone thought of her.

I watched her thin, petite body animate every detail of her new eye candy, as her big green eyes expressed her emotions. She wasn't drop-dead gorgeous or model material, but her personality definitely put her in that category.

She tied her long, wavy black hair up in a ponytail and proceeded to detail every bit of this new guy in her life. But I was still thinking about Tristen.

The third period bell rang when I realized that I was starving. Good. Just one more hour before lunch.

As I opened my locker to switch out my books for Calculus next period, I wondered what Mom packed for me. Breakfast was huge, but lunch was not much smaller. Normally, Mom would pack two sandwiches—roast beef and ham on a croissant with pickles, lettuce, homemade ketchup (yes, homemade ketchup!), onions, and mustard—a thermos of her famous pomegranate juice, chips, and a banana.

There was not much that I enjoyed doing more than eating. All of my memories revolved around food. Mom was always cooking. She always made sure she had breakfast, lunch, and dinner for me every day. I realized that I was getting older and that I should be able to cook for myself. But let's be honest, what teenager didn't like to be spoiled with food? She definitely spoiled me. She always encouraged me to try the different recipes she would conjure up in her head or find on the Internet. And they always seemed to be delicious. I often wondered why she chose to be in the medical field when she could have been a chef.

As I closed my locker door, I caught sight of a figure standing behind it and I almost peed my pants.

I grabbed my chest. "Oh, God! You scared me!" My brain hadn't yet registered it was Tristen until I heard his deep, intoxicating voice.

"Sorry. I shouldn't have been a creep hiding behind your locker door like that," he said with a laugh.

Oh. My. God. Between my heart racing from being startled and Tristen speaking to me, I thought I might just pass out.

"No, it's fine. So...what's up?"

Just play it off, Grace.

"Are you going to Calculus right now?" he asked, resting against the locker.

"Yeah," I whispered. I could feel my armpits beginning to sweat. I prayed it wouldn't show.

"I'm sort of not doing well in that class. Math was never my favorite subject."

"Oh, yeah," I breathed out, followed by a ridiculously loud giggle. Jeez, I knew I sounded like an idiot. I wasn't sure if I had asked a question or made a statement.

"So, in order for me to stay on the swim team, I really need to bring my grade up," he admitted with a shameful look. "I was wondering if maybe you could tutor me. I'm usually free on Thursdays, if that's okay with you?"

Did he ask me what I thought he just asked me? What should I say? I mean, Tristen—the most attractive, sexy, gorgeous guy in school—was asking *me* to tutor *him*. Was I sweating? I felt kind of numb. Would I go to his house to help him study? Or would he come to my house? Oh my God. I really needed to clean my room! Wait! Would he come into my bedroom? Well, that would be a little slutty of me. I wouldn't let him come into my bedroom on our first date! Ha! This wouldn't be a date, would it? Oh God. I could smell the sweat under my arms...

"Um...Grace?" He looked confused.

My vision finally came back, and I could see the baffled expression on his face. "Oh, sorry. So you need help? Yeah I can—"

"Tristen! I was waiting for you by my locker! What are you doing...with Granny-panty?"

And there she was, perfect Sonny Westwood. She stomped her way in between us, throwing her arm around his neck. I flinched when she tossed her perfect hair into my face. "Can we go? We're gonna be late."

"Yeah, I was just asking Grace for some help with Calculus."

I gazed down at my feet when she turned to look at me. "Why? Sweetie, I don't think she knows enough about Calculus to help you. I mean, is she even smart?" she asked, giving an awful duck face.

"Well, she does have an A in the class and she loves math." He smiled and glanced over at me. I did love math. How did he know that?

"Yeah, I do love math," I whispered under my breath.

"What? Did you say something, Granny?" she asked.

"Yeah," Tristen answered for me. "She said she loves math. Come on. I have to get to class." His patience with her seemed to have run out. "Grace, will you meet me here on Thursday after school?"

Okay, I assumed he wanted an answer now.

"Um, yeah...yes. Thursday. Sounds good," I said, heart still racing. Sonny whipped her head back around to Tristen, this time leaving the taste of her shampoo in my mouth. I quickly tried to get it out. I couldn't see her face, but I imagined it was not pleasant. She was probably cursing him with her eyes, and I was almost positive she was cursing me in her head.

He grabbed her hand and they walked away.

Thursday. Wait, what was today? Okay, Tuesday. Tuesday?

I stood by my locker, trying to understand what just happened.

In the two years that Tristen had been at Middleton, we had never really spoken. Once, we had bumped into each other in the breezeway outside. He had turned to me and said, "Oh, sorry." I had nodded and just kept on my way. Then, last year, he asked me what pages of *Catcher in the Rye* were we supposed to read for homework in English class. I mumbled off some chapters before burying my head in my book. But other than that, we never really spoke. Sonny snatched him before anyone could even have a chance. Since then, he had been with her nonstop.

What was it about her? I understood she was attractive, wealthy, and...well, that was pretty much it. She was not a nice person. And although she did have great grades, I refused to believe it was due to her hard work. Her parents probably paid the school off. And to be honest, not being smart should bring down the attractive level a notch. But I shouldn't judge. Maybe underneath all of that makeup, blonde hair, designer clothes, and powerful-because-my-parents-are-wealthy-and-successful exterior, she was a decent and sensitive person.

Probably not.

Calculus could not have taken any longer. As I sat in class, listening to Mrs. Turner explain the derivative of parametric equations, I watched Tristen two rows over and three desks in front of me struggling to understand what she was saying. He really seemed to need help. I fantasized about what Thursday was going to be like. Maybe his parents would be working, so we would be alone. Where would we be studying? His living room? His dining room? His bedroom? What does his bedroom look like? Does he have pictures of Sonny everywhere? Were we only going to talk about Calculus?

I realized this could be the first time that I was going to be completely alone with a guy that I truly had a crush on. Don't get me wrong, I had been on a date or two. I wasn't completely deprived of boy-girl contact. I had a boyfriend in ninth grade. During freshmen year, there was a guy named Josh who was very cute and funny. We started dating, and then we broke up like two weeks later. It was completely PG-13. We only kissed on the lips once. So, I never actually really kissed someone before. My mom would say that making out with boys was not ladylike. She would say that sticking a tongue down a boy's throat was vulgar and kisses should be polite and sweet.

I got what she was saying. Whenever I would see kissing scenes in movies, or when Phoebe's making out with one of her boy toys, it kind of grossed me out. It seemed sloppy and like it would just be awkward.

I was curious to know how Tristen kissed, though. I wondered if he was gentle. He was different than all of the other horny jocks that ran around school trying to be with every cute girl they saw. When he hung out with Sonny and the clique, you could tell being popular wasn't his entire life. He didn't strive to be part of the clique like everyone else did. Sonny's minions and all of the other wannabes tried desperately to be a part of the popular crowd. But not Tristen.

He had a presence about him that seemed humbling, down-to-earth. It was nice.

But I knew I ran the risk of getting to know him and learning that he was the complete opposite of my expectations. Let's face it—he was dating Perfect Sonny, he was popular, and he was a jock. They couldn't all be the same, right?

THE REQUEST

THE LUNCH BELL RANG, breaking me out of my thoughts of Tristen. I grabbed my lunch out of my locker and went to meet Phoebe in the courtyard at our usual table. I walked outside into the breezeway, breathing in the fresh air. It was a gorgeous Fall day.

Middleton High School was a very small, one-story facility. It was shaped like a U, with the cafeteria and courtyard in the middle. Phoebe and I always chose to sit outside on days like these to enjoy the weather this time of year.

When I reached our table, she was flirting with a short, googly-eyed sophomore.

"So, if you can just do that for me, that would be amazeballs," she said as she grazed his hand with her fingertips and batted her eyes.

"Uh...no problem. I'll...uh...slip it into your locker tomorrow morning before class," he said nervously. As he got up and walked away, I gave her a look.

"What?" she asked innocently.

"What's that poor little sophomore doing for you, Phoebe?"

"Oh, Grace. Don't judge. He's going to do my paper for me." She shrugged.

"Phoebe," I said in a tone to let her know that I was a tad bit disappointed. "Why? You are so good at writing."

"I know. It's just that I have to work tonight."

"I thought you were off?"

"Well, I decided to work because...I need the money." She was so sure about her lie, but I could see straight through it.

"You mean, you need to work with that guy. Phoebe, just because he's cute does not mean that you can slack off at school. You know we're finishing up our college applications next week."

"I know, I know. It'll be fine. So, what did your mom make you today? Whatever it is, I want some. I'm so hungry, and they're serving mystery burgers in the cafeteria. Blah." She crinkled her nose as if she smelled something terrible.

"Yeah, here. You can have half my roast beef." I tore a piece off and gave it to her, but deep down it killed me. I was so hungry, which I always seemed to be at this time of the day.

"Why does your mom make so much lunch for you?" she asked, biting into the juicy roast beef sandwich. "I mean, you're like a toothpick. I never understand where it all goes."

"I don't know," I responded with a mouthful. "You know I always eat a lot. Mom says I have always been like this. I just love food. It's, like, the greatest invention." I giggled. And it was true. To me, food was just heaven. I woke up looking forward to eating. It didn't just fill me up or satisfy my hunger. It made me feel...good. I was always full of energy after I ate.

Sometimes, I even thought it would make me physically look better. Mom said it's because of all the energy I felt after I ate—kind of like when you get a good night's sleep. But sometimes, I swear that I could look in the mirror after a good meal and see my face glowing. Food and I...we had a special relationship.

"So, Phoebe," I said before I took my next bite. "Tristen was at my locker last period."

"You're shitting me," Phoebe whispered loudly as she leaned closer to me from across the table. "What did he want?"

I took another bite and quickly chewed and swallowed before I answered. "He wants me to tutor him. He wants me to meet him Thursday at my locker so that we can go study."

Wow. It really sank in right when I said that out loud. I almost couldn't swallow.

"Are you kidding me? Well, so, are you going?"

"Of course I'm going," I practically yelled. I glanced around to make sure no one else was listening. I really didn't want anyone else to know. No one really knew how much I liked Tristen except Phoebe. I had mentioned it to my mother a few times over the years, too. But I didn't want to be known as that girl in school who had no life because she fantasized about the popular boy. Not to mention, I didn't want Sonny finding out. God only knew how much harder she would make my life. I was sure she'd get every chance she got to rub their relationship in my face.

"Phoebe, I can't *not* go. I mean, he needs my help. I'm going to help him learn Calculus." I couldn't believe my own lie much less think Phoebe believed it.

"G, I know you're freaking out right now about what you're going to wear and what's going to happen. It's fine. I'll dress you." She gave me a matter-of-fact look.

"What? No, you're most certainly not dressing me. I don't want to look like a hooker," I said, trying to make it sound like a joke when really, I was being serious.

Phoebe didn't look like a prostitute per se. She just chose to wear clothing that revealed her belly ring and exceptionally large boobs. She had a great body, don't get me wrong. She was very curvaceous and proportioned well. It was just that her boobs were bigger than they should have been for her size, and she knew it. And she loved it. And so did every other guy in school.

"I'll figure out what to wear."

"Okay," she said as if to warn me. "Just remember that guys cannot resist a girl who shows a little tummy and cleavage. At least wear a little bit of makeup for me." She pouted.

"No, guys like it when *you* show a little tummy and cleavage. You know I don't feel comfortable about that." And it was true, I really didn't. My mom never had to worry about me leaving the house with not enough clothing on. I always felt extremely awkward in midriffs and hiked-up skirts. Not that I was ashamed of my body—except my boobs. I was thin, with a natural olive complexion, and had somewhat of a curvy figure. And I certainly did not judge Phoebe for dressing the way she did. If you had it, flaunt it. I would just prefer to dress in comfort, which meant jeans and a T-shirt.

I would dress up when the occasion called for it. I wasn't sure if this was the occasion, though. Studying Calculus did not exactly scream miniskirt and a halter top. Then again, everything changes when it's studying Calculus with the hottest guy in school.

The next three periods seemed way too long. My day was completely complicated by my earlier encounter with Tristen. It should have been a totally amazing day, but my impending date with him on Thursday had me a little worried. I worried that I wouldn't know what else to talk about besides Calculus. I wasn't normally shy, but when it came to Tristen, I forgot the whole concept of words and how to use them. I was also worried about Sonny.

For some strange reason, Sonny had chosen to hate my whole existence. I never understood exactly why she chose me to crucify, but she had this unnatural desire to treat me as if I were the scum on her bathroom walls. Well, I was pretty positive she didn't have scum on the walls of her enormous mansion, but something along those lines. I had known Sonny as long as I had known Phoebe, since elementary school, and she never liked me. To be honest, I guess I felt the same way. The only difference was that I disliked her because of how she treated me. She just disliked me for no apparent reason.

I knew she was fuming about Tristen asking me for help, and I worried that she would scheme to make my life a living hell for doing it. Or worse. She could show up. I guess I should just be prepared because I cannot let Thursday *not* happen. I would be a total idiot.

School was only about four blocks away from home. When I first started Middleton High, Mom offered to drive me, but I chose to walk with Phoebe every morning and afternoon. Over the past few months, since Phoebe got her new job at the mall, she had been leaving school to go straight there on most of the days. So, I had been walking alone. It didn't bother me much, though.

I enjoyed walking. Being outside was one of my favorite things to do. The scent of the sun on my clothes, the smell of the trees, and the feeling of fresh air making its way into my lungs exhilarated me.

It made me feel alive and happy to be alive. My senses always seemed heightened, and I swear I could smell a flowerbed from a mile away. Anytime I tried to express how nature made me feel, I would just get lost in the words. My mom would only smile at me while Phoebe would say that I was weird. So, I learned to keep my love of nature to myself and enjoy it quietly.

I got home at my usual three o'clock time. When I walked up the driveway, I was surprised to see my mom home early from work.

"Hey, Mom!" I yelled as I opened the front door.

"Hi, sweetheart! I'm in the kitchen!"

Of course she was. I threw my bookbag on the couch and went into the kitchen to greet her with a kiss.

"I thought you had to work late tonight."

"I thought I did, too. You know I try not to work late unless it's necessary. I would rather be home with you. So how was school today?" she asked as she thumbed through the mail at the kitchen table. I went straight to the fridge to get some pomegranate goodness.

"Oh, you know. It was school." I couldn't help but smile.

"Did you learn anything fun? Oh, and honey, how did you like your lunch today?"

"Well, it's funny that you ask—"

Mom popped her head up to glare at me from across the table. "You didn't like it?" she asked, almost as if she were horrified. "Gracie, did you eat lunch today?"

"Mom, yes. I ate lunch. Lunch was great. I always eat your lunch. You know that," I reassured her. She took a deep breath and went back to the mail. Mom was very sensitive about her cooking.

I loved her food and never had a problem with it, but if I didn't like it for some reason, she would become completely crazy and try to perfect what she had made. I thought it was a bit OCD, but Mom's passion for cooking was important to her, and I supported that. Sometimes I wondered if it was what she did to forget about Dad leaving. Maybe it was her way of coping. I could never ask, though. Jack was a sore subject.

"Anyway, something great actually did happen today," I said. "Remember the boy that I really like at school?" I didn't think that she forgot him, really. It was the only time I had ever confided in my mother regarding a crush. And it was only because she overheard Phoebe and me dishing about which guys at school were the cutest.

"Oh, yes. Tristen, is it? Yes, I remember," she said as she continued to write in her checkbook.

"Well, I'm going to be tutoring him. He needs help with Calculus." I pulled a chair out to join her at the antique wooden kitchen table. Most of the things in our house were antique—Mom had an interest in old things.

She smiled softly, not lifting her head from her checkbook. "That's great, Gracie. Isn't he dating that Sam girl?"

My ridiculous grin faded. Why would she burst my bubble? Didn't she know how much I liked him?

"Um...yeah." I couldn't help shifting uncomfortably in my chair. "Her name is Sonny. She's perfect," I mumbled under my breath.

Mom must have sensed the slight disappointment in my voice because she looked up at me. "Gracie, I didn't mean to hurt your feelings, sweetie, but he is dating someone. Don't you think it would be inappropriate for you to act on how you feel for him? Do you think it would even be a good idea to tutor him, knowing how you feel?"

Why was she trying to rain on my parade? I stared at her for a moment, letting what she just said seep into my mind.

"I guess you're right," I said through clenched teeth. "I won't have a problem tutoring him, though. He really does need the help, and it'll make me feel good to help him." I picked up my glass and stood. "I think I'm gonna go listen to some music."

I could see a little bit of guilt in Mom's eyes before I turned to walk out of the room. "Okay, dear."

I went upstairs into my bedroom, grabbed my iPod, and threw myself back onto the bed. Why was she being so uptight about this? I mean, I got what she was saying. Okay, he had a girlfriend. And she was perfect. But that didn't mean that I couldn't like him. Almost every girl in school liked him. And I was sure almost every girl in the greater New Orleans area liked him, too. What was so wrong with that?

As I lay there thinking, I realized that Mom didn't really like me dating Josh, either. I remembered I had to beg her to let me go on a date with him. The other times we hung out, I had to sneak out to see him. She would have killed me if she knew that I kissed him.

This was ridiculous. I was seventeen years old, almost a college student, and very mature for my age. Anyway, Tristen was dating the epitome of perfection. I doubted that he would want anything less than perfect at this point. And I was way less than perfect.

Then again, maybe he was tired of perfect.

I could hear my stomach begin to rumble. I needed food. Soon.

After listening to a little music while I did my Calculus, Civics, and English homework, I nearly began running downstairs when the scent of sizzling fajitas reached my smell receptors. That aroma made me feel like I hadn't eaten in months.

"Gracie, dinner is—" Mom yelled right as she watched me tumble onto the kitchen floor. "Grace! Are you okay?" she asked frantically, bending over to help me up.

I shuffled to my feet. I couldn't help but giggle a little. I wasn't normally clumsy, but every now and then I would get dizzy if I felt too hungry.

"I'm fine, Mom. Just hungry."

I made my way to the table where steak fajitas, black beans with sausage and rice, fried little banana thingies, and chips and salsa were awaiting my starving mouth.

"Mom, it looks so good," I said with a growl after swallowing a mouthful of saliva.

"Well, eat up. You need food right now," she demanded. She pulled out the chair across the table in front of me and sat down. I couldn't be polite. I had to start that very moment.

"So, Gracie, I was thinking about our conversation earlier," she said while placing her napkin on her lap. I swallowed hard. "I didn't mean to sound...insensitive." Sincerity swept her face. "I just don't want you to get hurt, honey."

I swallowed hard again, wondering why she would think I'd get hurt. I got that he was in love with Miss Perfectly Perfect, and I didn't expect us to be together after one study date.

I continued to eat the delectably delicious steak fajitas.

"It's just that, he has a girlfriend. He may not think of you in the way you want him to. Not to mention, if he does, you could come in between them and cause a big mess."

I managed to keep the fork out of my mouth for a moment. "Mom, I know that. I'm not expecting anything from him. Besides, Sonny hates me."

"She hates you? Why?"

I shrugged off her question. I didn't want to get into that.

"Well, I just worry. Anyway, you should be focusing on your college applications," she said before finally picking up her fork to eat. How could she resist digging in from the smell alone?

I nodded, and we continued to eat in silence.

After dinner, Mom sat in the bay window reading a book, and I went upstairs to surf the Internet. I'd say surf, but really, just jump on Facebook to check out what my friends were doing. That was the great thing about social media. You could be nosy without actually being nosy. People wanted you to know what they were doing. It always amazed me how people would post updates about their lives every thirty minutes.

Going to the movies with so-and-so. Getting my ticket for the movie. Movie is about to start. Just got out of the movie. On my way home from the movie. Sitting on my toilet thinking about the movie.

Really?

I changed into my pajama pants and my mom's old Berkeley University T-shirt, flopped onto the bed, opened my laptop and signed in. There was a friend request awaiting my approval when the homepage popped up. I clicked it, sure that it would be some random person who was a friend of a sister's boyfriend's best friend of a friend that I currently had on my friends list. In other words, someone I didn't care to be friends with.

Tristen Miles is awaiting your approval.

What? I rubbed my eyes to make sure that I was not temporarily blind and only envisioning what I'd read. He was asking me to be his friend? My initial reaction was to wonder why. Why now? Were we friends now because I agreed to tutor him?

I stared at my laptop, recognizing that there may be some consequences to this. If I accepted his request to be friends on a social network, there was the slight possibility that I might end up wasting too much time in my day checking to see what he did the night before, which would grant me a stalker status. Also, there was the high possibility that Sonny would see we were friends and it would add fuel to the fire she already wanted to set me on.

I squinted at the tiny picture next to the request—he and Sonny wearing sombreros at what seemed to be some kind of Mexican restaurant.

He liked Mexican food. So did I.

I began to wonder what else he liked. If he cherished food as much as I did, or loved horrors movies, or if he liked comic books, or enjoyed walking in the park on a beautiful day.

I held my finger up to my mouth and squeezed my nail between my teeth.

Grace, just do it! my subconscious yelled.

I lowered my finger down to the mouse pad, hovered the cursor over the ACCEPT option, and after about ten seconds, tapped the pad. There. We were friends. That wasn't so bad.

I resisted the urge to scan through his profile. I closed my laptop and set it on the nightstand next to my bed. I flipped the lamp off and cuddled up in my blankets, wondering if my decision was smart. Who knew, maybe this would be the start of a great friendship.

Mom's words slowly crept into my thoughts, making me cringe. *He may not think of you in the way you want him to.* Did I expect anything more? Would this decision to help him study be the beginning of disappointments and hurt feelings?

Was I being dramatic? I mean, we were just going to study together. No biggie.

THE HUNGER

THE NEXT MORNING, I awoke to the smell of bacon and pancakes, and I was sure much more. I changed into a gray camisole, jeans, and Converse, and then threw on a brown-and-white flannel shirt with the buttons undone. In the bathroom, I tied my hair up into a messy bun. I mentally nitpicked at all my flaws in the mirror, touched the bags under my eyes, and wondered if it was time for me to begin wearing makeup. Maybe Phoebe was right—makeup might make guys think I was a little more attractive. I didn't think I was ugly, but I could use a little help.

I grazed my fingers over the tiny freckles scattered around my nose and cheeks, and then down to my pale, full lips. Sonny wore makeup. Maybe Tristen liked that.

"Gracie! Breakfast is ready, my dear!" Mom yelled from downstairs.

Still staring, I dropped my hand down to my side, letting out a small sigh. Tomorrow. I would put some makeup on tomorrow.

After attending to my hygiene duties, I grabbed my bookbag and slowly walked downstairs. I was starving. Normally, I would be dashing down the stairs, two steps at a time, but I was feeling a bit lethargic this morning.

I devoured my incredibly large but scrumptious breakfast, kissed Mom on the cheek, and hopped out the door to meet Phoebe for our walk to school. My lethargy quickly dissipated after the fantastic breakfast.

School was the same. Between classes, Phoebe indulged in telling me of her almost-work date with...oh wait, I finally got a name: Eric. From what I understood, she and Eric flirted continuously while at work—giving each other sexy looks and briefly making contact as they walked near each other. She liked him more than a lot and was waiting for the right time to ask him out. I did envy Phoebe's lack of worry about being rejected. I wondered that if Tristen was single, would I have enough guts to ask him out? Doubtful.

The school day ended with an excited Phoebe rushing to get to work, a malicious look from Sonny, and a slight smile from Tristen. I was used to Phoebe and Sonny, but when I saw the corners of Tristen's mouth slowly turn up when our eyes met in the breezeway after the final bell, I had a mini stroke. If it wasn't for the rumbling that came from my stomach, I probably would have frozen in the moment. But I was starving. So, I smiled a gentle smile, lowering my head down like a shy little girl, and rushed to get home to some food.

On my walk home, I sucked in the aroma of the Fall air. I admired the gardens that outlined the sidewalks, allowing my fingertips to graze the blooming flowers fighting their way out of the iron fences that surrounded them. The houses in my neighborhood were the old French-style type. They were mostly two stories, brick, with stairs leading up to the front doors and balconies above them. There was a charm about them, warm and homey. The neighbors were friendly but mostly kept to themselves. They were either really old—lived in the same house for decades—or really young, newly started families. There really wasn't an in-between. I wanted to raise my own family here one day.

I briefly wondered what Tristen's plans for the future were.

When I reached my driveway, I noticed a black Mercedes Benz parked behind my mother's car. Who would be here? We never had company.

I walked through the front door to find my mom on the couch, facing someone sitting on the loveseat. I could only see the back of his head.

They stood up immediately.

"Grace. Hi, honey," she greeted. She smiled, but it seemed to be hiding concern. The man stood up with her and turned to face me. He was tall, clean-shaven, with gold-rimmed glasses and black hair. "This is Dr. Walker. He is a...an old colleague."

Dr. Walker extended his hand out to me. "Hi, Grace. You can call me Mark." His smile was magnificent, but I didn't feel comfortable calling him Mark.

I reached to shake his hand, a little shocked that we had a guest over, and even more shocked that he was so cute, in a doctor kind of way.

"Hi," I smiled back.

"Wow! You look so much like your mother. Veronica, you didn't tell me she was as beautiful as you."

My mom's cheeks turned a shade of pink.

"I have heard so much about you. Your mother was just singing your praises."

My mom quickly added, "Well, she is a wonderful daughter." She looked a bit nervous, which was odd to me because Mom was normally very confident about everything.

"It's been a long time since we have spoken, so I just wanted to let him know how blessed I was to have you." She smiled nervously and shifted her eyes over to him.

"Okay," I said, not sure of what else to say. We stood there for a moment in awkward silence.

"Um...Gracie, if you could just give Dr. Walker and me a few more minutes..."

"No, yeah, that's fine. I have a ton of homework to do, anyway." Thank God. It was beginning to feel too uncomfortable.

"Gotta get that homework done," Dr. Walker added. "Do you like to study? What are your favorite subjects?" he asked with curiosity in his tone.

"Pretty much everything. Math is my thing, though. Mom always wonders how I'm so good at it."

"Well, your mother wasn't known as the mathematician around the office. But, you do well?"

"Yeah. I just like it, I guess. I never really thought about it." Why *did* I like math? It came naturally to me, I'd guess. I never struggled as much as, say, Phoebe did. Most of the kids in our school dreaded math, but I didn't mind it.

"Well, good for you. Keep up the good work. Have you been feeling okay?"

I looked at my mom, and it was as if she were burning a hole through his head with her eyes. Was she upset that he was making conversation with me?

"Um...yes. I have been well. Just tired from so much studying. Well, I should get to it." I smiled and politely excused myself from the living room.

As I walk up the stairs, I could hear a whisper and barely make out my mom saying, "...don't think you should be asking her those types of questions."

I entered my room and shut the door quietly, wondering what that was supposed to mean. Why couldn't he ask me those types of questions? What alarmed me even more was Mom's nervousness. I had never heard of a Dr. Mark Walker before. Mom had never mentioned him. And why would he ask me if I have been feeling well?

I'd guess it was a doctor thing. Mom used to be a doctor. A surgeon. She always asked me how I was feeling. Maybe it was in their nature to make sure people were not feeling ill.

My stomach made a loud rumble, but I really didn't want to go back downstairs into the awkwardness. Maybe my mom liked Dr. Walker and wanted some time alone with him. That would be interesting. Mom had only been on a handful of dates—that I knew of. She said she would rather spend her time with me and that it was too late in her life to be dating. But maybe she had reconsidered.

I threw myself on my bed and stared at the ceiling. Thoughts of tomorrow's study date circled my mind, and before I knew it, my eyes grew heavier.

It's suddenly late at night and I'm walking slowly through an empty field, with only the moonlight guiding my way. There's heavy fog low at my feet, obstructing my view of the ground. I feel nervous, scared, not sure of what I'm doing. I walk and walk as the fog grows heavier and heavier at my feet. I feel dizzy and hungry. So, so hungry. I can't smell anything. My vision is blurred. But I can vaguely hear a crunching sound as my feet step forward.

I stop and bend to see what I'm stepping on, but still can't make out anything. I touch the ground, only to feel the soft soil. I flail my arms around, pushing the fog to either side of me. I push and push until suddenly, there is something. I bend down closer to get a better view, only to see what looks like a finger pointing straight up. I stare for a moment, not understanding why this finger is protruding out of the soggy mud. I become curious and want to touch it.

As I slowly bring my fingertips toward it, it twitches. Once, twice, three times. I reach down closer, still curious. I don't stand up. I don't run away. The finger begins to move, grabbing on to the edge. Another finger emerges. Then another, and another, until five fingers are in the air. I am mesmerized, frozen in time.

The hand begins to move again, clawing into the soil now, pulling the earth farther and farther down. A wrist emerges, then an arm. The skin is pale and smells of rot, with greenish, black blisters and bruises. I can see a balding head beginning to crown through the surface. The few strands of hair on the blistering scalp are thin, long, and gray. As the head slowly makes its way out and a face becomes visible, I start to realize that it looks familiar. She looks familiar. There are heavy bags under her eyes, tiny freckles scattered on her nose and cheeks, and pale, full lips. She's me.

My eyes sprung open as I lay still in my bed. I stared at the ceiling, wondering why I was not a crying mess from the terrible vision of myself I'd just witnessed in my sleep. When I tried to turn my head to get a glimpse of the time on my nightstand, I winced at the ache radiating from my neck to my toes.

I struggled to lift myself up into a sitting position, realizing at the same time that the sheets were wet. My forehead and entire body were covered in sweat. I reached over to flick on the lamp. The light burned my retinas, so I flicked it back off quickly. I glanced over at the clock, squinting and struggling to read the time. I could barely see. It was blurry, but after focusing for a moment, the clock read 3 a.m.

I slowly maneuvered myself out of the bed, trying desperately not to move too fast. Honestly, I couldn't if I wanted to. Stumbling into my bathroom, I felt my way to the toilet seat to relieve myself, only to find that I really didn't need to. Instead, I stood up, decided not to turn the light on, and tried to focus my eyes in the darkness until I found the mirror. Looking into it and gripping the edge of the sink at the same time to keep from falling back, the silhouette of my reflection finally appeared. I decided to flick the light on to get a better view, wincing when the illumination felt like shards of glass inside my pupils. I gasped.

My face was almost unrecognizable. The bags under my eyes were sagging down into my caved-in cheeks. My lips were no longer full but were drooping down, as if someone threw a punch right into them. My eyes were black and sunken in, with veins protruding and pulsating out of the corners. I lifted my head to get a better view of my neck, only to see my skin seemed wrinkled and aged. My hair was thinner, straighter, lifeless.

After noticing my best feature was not my best, I couldn't look any longer. I felt too tired and sick to go get Mom, so I grabbed my cell phone and dialed her number the best I could.

"Hello?" she asked sleepily but alarmed.

I could barely get a word to come out of my mouth.

"Gracie?" Her voice slowly became frantic.

Before I could get enough strength to let out the first two letters of a word, she flung open the door to my room, finding me on the floor near my bed. I couldn't make it all the way.

"Gracie!" She ran over to me, bending down and wrapping her arms around me to try to lift me up off the floor. I cried out in pain, sensing every inch of my bones feeling as though they were going to crack. I felt light against her, as if she could easily throw me over her shoulder.

"Sweetie, we have to get some food in you. I should have never let you sleep without dinner! I knew this was going to happen!" Her voice broke with disappointment.

She walked me down the hall and down the stairs, one step at a time. We got into the kitchen where she gingerly set me down at the kitchen table. I slumped over to the side, unable to keep myself balanced. The room was spinning now and agonizing pain shot through every joint, muscle, bone, and inch my of skin. I heaved over when I felt the dreadful ache in my stomach. It felt as though I was hungry, nauseous, and had the worst case of food poisoning all at the same time.

"It's okay, honey. Just try to hold on for one more second. I'm going to give you exactly what you need."

As soon as she let me go, she flew over to the fridge, taking out every container full of food we had. I wanted to yell at her. How could I possibly eat? It felt like my body was about to turn into soup and splash all over the kitchen floor. I needed to go to the hospital. What was my mom thinking? She was a doctor, for crying out loud!

The words couldn't even form in my throat. I watched her pop every container open and start to bring them over to the table. As soon as I smelled the first whiff of leftover food, my eyes darted over to it. I began to breathe heavily, and all I could think about was the food in front of me.

Suddenly, the pain was out of my mind, and though I could still feel my bones becoming more tender and brittle by the second, I didn't care. I sat still, focusing on the containers.

"Okay, Gracie. Here you go. You can eat."

I was aware that my mom had been done pulling out every bit of ration we had in the refrigerator, but I didn't care. I knew she was speaking to me, but I didn't care. I kept my eyes in one place.

"Gracie! You need to eat! Now!" she yelled desperately.

At that same moment, my hands involuntarily dug into the container and began a shoveling motion into my mouth. I wasn't even sure that I was chewing. The smell whirled around my head, colliding with the taste of what I could have sworn to be the first time

I had ever tried food. It was like I didn't understand what I was doing, but at the same time, understood everything. I wanted that food. I needed that food. Every cell in my body was screaming at me to eat the food.

I couldn't stop. I wasn't sure I wanted to stop. The taste was so savory. I could feel every morsel enter my mouth and slowly make its way down my esophagus and into my stomach. I could feel my stomach welcoming the deliciousness, digesting it, and absorbing the nutrients into my bloodstream. My body slowly awoke with each bite.

I threw the empty containers to the side when I was finished, continuing on to the next without hesitation. I couldn't look away. I had to protect what was in front of me. It was mine.

It was when I devoured the very last container that I felt I had enough control to stop.

"There you go, sweetheart. How do you feel?"

I suddenly missed my mom's voice.

I looked up at her, and then down at the empty containers strewn around the kitchen. I glanced down at myself covered in a mess of crumbs and sticky sauce and an array of colors. My gaze returned to my mother, and embarrassment and guilt were among the many emotions flowing through me. I wanted to cry.

"No. No, sweetie," she said softy, sensing my humility. She walked over to my side of the table, sliding her arm over my shoulder as she took in the messy sight.

"Mom, I'm so sorry. I just…I didn't know…" I couldn't finish my sentence, overwhelmed with what I saw.

"Gracie." She turned my face toward hers with a finger under my chin. "It's okay. You feel better, don't you?"

I nodded, too embarrassed to even speak.

"Good. That's all that matters, baby. We fixed it. You were just really hungry. It happens." The corners of her mouth turned up, easing my emotions somewhat. But my emotions were still all over the place.

I wasn't quite sure of what just happened. I knew that I woke up from a nap—more than a nap, obviously. I missed dinner, which I had done in the past. But I had never, not even a tiny bit, felt this hungry. I got dizzy or tired from time to time, but never to this extreme. Never to the point where my body felt as though it were becoming mush or slowly deteriorating. Never to the point where I had to eat thirty pounds of food to regain any sense of strength back. And certainly, never to the point where I had absolutely no control over what I was doing.

"Come on, Gracie. Let's get you into the shower." Mom seemed mysteriously calm despite the fact that her daughter just consumed almost every item the refrigerator could hold.

I looked back at the disaster as we made our way up the stairs. Yup, pretty much everything in the refrigerator.

Mom helped me shower, as I was still a little distraught from the whole situation. My body felt amazing, though—like it never even happened. But my mind was in other places. The dream, the terrible stab-like pains exuding through my body, the hollowness of my face, Mom's guilt of not waking me to have dinner, the spinning, the sweet and satisfying taste of the leftovers, the aftermath...Tristen.

"Mom, what's today?" I asked, suddenly feeling like I forgot something, similar to when one leaves on a road trip and swears they may have left the oven on.

"It's Thursday morning, sweetie," she said as she wrapped the towel around my naked body.

"It's what?" I threw the towel on the floor and rushed to my closet.

"Grace, what's wrong?" she asked with concern.

"It's Thursday! I have a date with Tristen, and I haven't picked out what I'm going to wear!"

I knew I seemed a bit melodramatic at the moment, but this was important. I actually worked it out in my head over the past two days. There was a lot of truth in Phoebe's theory of boys being attracted to chicks who show off a little. I wasn't completely sure that Tristen had even thought of me in the way I thought of him. I wasn't completely sure if all of my stress over him was even worth it. But, if I were to dress a little...sexy, his reaction would speak volumes. If once he saw me, he didn't stare or try to check me out or employ any kind of eyebrow raises, then I'd know that he just wasn't interested.

But if he did do any of those things, then I would at least know that I had piqued his interest. I would at least know that he didn't think I was just some nerd tutoring him.

"You have a date with him?" she asked as she sat on the edge of my bed. I knew she wouldn't like this.

"Well, it's not a date, Mom. I told you, I'm just tutoring him," I said, rummaging through my closet.

"You said 'date'. Grace, I told you I didn't think this was a good idea. Why doesn't he just ask the teacher to help him?"

I shot her a look. "Because, Mom, he asked me. Why is this such a bad thing? I want to help him. He asked me because I am smart. Why can't I share that? Why can't I do something nice for someone?"

I thought that my little daring remark might finally make her understand how important this was to me, but I knew my mother better than that. She was never wrong about her intuitions. And deep down inside, I knew she was right.

She sat in silence for a few moments. I turned back around in desperate search of something even remotely sexy. My wardrobe consisted of comfortable, laid-back attire. This was going to be tough.

"You know what, Gracie? You're right."

I froze.

"You should be able to help someone who's in need. But you'll have to tutor him here."

I swung around to face her. "Well, what if he wants me to go to his house?"

"Then you can tell him to come here instead."

"Why are you so adamant about this? I get that you think this is a bad idea. To even be tutoring him when he has a girlfriend, but why must I be here?"

She stood up and walked over to me. She grabbed my face gently with both her hands.

"Because, Gracie, it *is* a bad idea. This situation has the potential of hurting someone. Someone *will* get hurt. You're becoming a woman, and soon you'll be making your own decisions. But as long as you're under my roof, I'll protect you from whatever I can. He will come here. And that is final."

She kissed me on my forehead and left my room.

If this moment were a cartoon, steam would be bursting out of my ears. How could she be so irrational? I was seventeen years old. I could absolutely make my own decisions. Mom had never been this way with me before.

Well, to be fair, I had never been in a situation like this before.

Maybe she did know what she was talking about. Maybe she had been-there-done-that when she was younger.

No. She was being ridiculous.

I glanced at the clock. I had an hour and a half before I should start getting ready for school. I continued on with my search for the right outfit. I settled on a tight-fitting, long-sleeved shirt, skinny jeans, and ankle boots with a slight heel. It was not a midriff or a cleavage-baring blouse, but it would have to do. I couldn't seem to allow myself to show too much skin. I didn't have the boobs, and I certainly didn't have the guts to let it all hang out like Phoebe did. With the way I was feeling at the moment, the necessity to be sexy left my mind.

I should have been exhausted with the morning that I had, but my body was totally normal. If anything, it was better. Mom didn't seem the least bit worried about my behavior in the kitchen. I would have to discuss that with her, but I was certainly keeping my distance for at least the rest of the day. I was pissed with her.

After throwing on my "sexy" outfit, I made my way to the bathroom to figure out what to do with my hair and makeup. Surely, I would need to cake on the makeup with the way I looked.

But a gasp escaped my throat when I glanced into the mirror. What happened to my face? It was not at all the horrific sight from earlier this morning. My color was back, and my eyes had returned to their natural shade of light brown, and I just looked...I looked... older?

The sprinkles of freckles around my nose were a shade darker, and I had creases around my mouth. I pinched my checks and they didn't spring back. I did have a rough night, and although I felt amazing, my appearance may not have caught up with me.

I shrugged it off and continued my quest to wow Tristen.

I made my way downstairs. Mom was in the kitchen cleaning up the mess I made.

"Gracie, are you hungry? I can make you some breakfast before you go."

It did sound tempting, but I informed her that I wasn't very hungry. How could I be?

"I'll just take some pomegranate juice," I said as I reached into the fridge.

"Okay, well I just made some last night. It's fresh."

Mom knew I was upset with her, so she didn't try to make much conversation. We had never really gotten into an argument before, and the tension between us felt uncomfortable.

We just needed some time to cool off, and then we would be fine.

THE BUFFET

"WHOA!" PHOEBE YELLED FROM across the street.

"It's that bad?" I asked, suddenly feeling extremely self-conscious.

"No! You look awesome, Grace Shelley!" She spun me around, smacking my butt when I made a full turn. "Tristen is so gonna love this."

"Well, I sort of took your advice."

"Your hair is flawless, as always. Good choice to leave it down. And you have makeup on? Oh my God. I can't wait to see Sonny's face."

I shrugged my shoulders. I tried to make myself believe I didn't care what Sonny thought, but deep down I wanted her to see what I was capable of.

"So, have you thought about how you're going to seduce him tonight?" she asked, adding a little shimmy to her step.

"Phoebe!" Blood flowed up to my cheeks. "Come on. It's not like that. He's just coming over to study. Nothing more."

"Right. Okay. You know he's gonna think you're hot, G. You're hotter than she is." Phoebe's matter-of-fact tone came back.

"Well, it doesn't matter, anyway. I'm not trying to seduce him or steal him away. He's a big boy, he can make his own decisions. I'm just trying to...help sway his decision a bit." And that was the truth. I didn't want to be known as The Boyfriend Snatcher, especially for my own safety from Sonny. I knew that if my plan to make him notice me did cause a break-up and he ended up with me, I ran the risk of gaining that title. But I wasn't necessarily stealing him from her. If he truly loved her, he would stay with her.

Was it worth the risk? Was it worth getting dirty looks from Sonny and her minions every day for the rest of the school year? I mean, I kind of already did. So what did I have to lose? I knew I would be gaining something...and it was something I had wanted for a long time.

"Oh, it's gonna work. Trust me."

I smiled.

"So, Eric asked me out, finally. It only took forever, but I think he might be a keeper," Phoebe said, hugging her textbook tight to her chest.

"You've said that before, and you ended up getting your heart broken."

"G, he is so amazing. He's a freshman in college, so he's much more mature than some of the idiots at our school. He's funny, hot, smart, hot, a great dresser...oh, did I say hot?"

I chuckled and stopped to face her. She was doe-eyed and clearly on cloud nine.

"Phoebe, I know. I have heard this before. But you always end up getting hurt. Maybe you should slow down before becoming exclusive. Find out who he really is instead of only focusing on the exterior."

"Grace, he is a good guy. I promise you."

I grabbed her shoulders and thought about shaking her. "I just worry about my best friend. I don't want anyone to hurt you, Phoebe. But you know if he does, I'm here. No matter how many times this has already happened."

She hugged me tight and whispered into my ear, "That's why you're my best friend."

My nerves were beginning to get the best of me when we came into view of our school. I couldn't decide if it was because I was nervous of Tristen's reaction or the rest of the school's reaction to my subtle makeover. I'd never made such an effort before. School dances were one thing. You were expected to show up in dresses and heels. You never really stood out because everyone was trying their hardest too. But this was not normal for me. The only people who truly made fashion statements were Sonny and her gang of clones.

Before we made our way up the main entrance, Phoebe turned toward me. "You look great, G. Don't worry. He will notice."

I smiled nervously and fought to believe her kind words.

"By the way, not only do you look great, but you look so...mature."

I frowned for a split second before forcing a smile. I had hoped no one would notice except me. I didn't exactly want to fill Phoebe in on what happened last night. It was a bad experience, and I didn't want to have to find a way to explain the only thing that made me feel better, which was ingesting an obscene amount of food. Not to mention, it was embarrassing.

"Are you trying to say I look old?" I asked, attempting to respond with humor.

"No way! Looking mature is actually really sexy."

"Well, let's hope Tristen thinks so, too."

The first half of the day was uneventful. To my surprise, Sonny and her Chain Gang were absent from their usual spot at the main entrance, where they critiqued everyone not worthy. And I hadn't seen Tristen all day. Anxiety began to set in when I realized that he may not be here today. Did he forget about our date? I mean...tutoring session? Did I make all of this effort for nothing? Was I an idiot to get my hopes up for something that I should have known was never going to happen?

I fidgeted and became flustered in my civics class during a debate. It was then that my thoughts became melodramatic and outlandish.

Was he purposely avoiding me? Was this whole asking-me-to-help-him-study thing a prank? Something from a movie where his best friend bets him to ask out the most desperate girl in school, who clearly has an enormous crush on him, only to humiliate her by pouring pig's blood all over her head in front of the whole school? Does Sonny have something to do with his disappearance? Was she mysteriously gone today, too, because she murdered him for asking me to help him?

During Calculus, I sat down at my desk and kept an eye on the door. Still no Tristen.

When the bell rang for lunch, those thoughts quickly dissipated. I was starving and I needed to eat.

I met Phoebe at our usual spot in the courtyard to begin my lunchtime feast. As we sat and ate, Phoebe beamed when she talked about Eric and his amazing body. I tried to listen but found myself nonchalantly scanning the courtyard for any sign of Tristen. My disappointment settled deeper and deeper. After she finished her gushing, she noticed my melancholy and reassured me that he will show to meet me after school. I appreciated her effort.

The final bell of the day rang, and I ominously made my way to my locker to collect my books. I opened my locker door and immediately wished I didn't have a mirror hanging inside. I stared at myself, feeling like the biggest loser alive. I suddenly felt the incredible urge to wash my face.

Stupid makeup! I hated wearing makeup! How could I have been so naive to think that caking on layers of processed, pimple-causing gunk would make the most popular, most beautiful guy at Middleton High like me?

I just knew it was too good to be true.

I grabbed a tissue and began to scrub. I couldn't scrub hard enough. It had to come off!

"Uh...Grace?" It was Tristen.

My heart skipped a beat. I stopped and peeked around my locker door.

"You okay?" he asked.

"Um, uh...yeah...I just...can you give me just one second?" I glanced in the mirror in horror. The stupid mascara was smeared all over my face! I looked like a raccoon! I desperately scrubbed until it hurt.

Then, Tristen grabbed my locker door and pushed it out of the way. "Listen, are you still available this afternoon?"

"Um...yeah, definitely. Did you still need help?" I asked, trying to make it seem like I wasn't eagerly awaiting his arrival all day long.

"I really do. We have a test tomorrow and I can't fail it. So, are you ready now?"

"Sure, I was just grabbing my books. Um...we can go to my house, if that's okay," I said, remembering my fight with Mom. I was still pissed.

"That sounds good, but my car's in the shop right now. Do you live far? I can get my mom to bring us."

"No, I live a few blocks away. We can walk."

The corners of his mouth turned up. "Absolutely, the weather is perfect for a walk."

It was as if my heart were melting like a candle slowly burning away the wax. I didn't respond and instead proceeded to grab my books and shut my locker door. When we exited the double doors into the breezeway, he suddenly stopped.

"Hey, you have something under your eye."

Before I could fathom up a lame excuse for the disaster on my face that he was obviously talking about, he raised his hand and gently glided his thumb under my eye. I stood still, unable to move. I watched his face as he gingerly tried to clean me up.

"There you go." His voice was soft. "Much better."

His arm fell to his side, and we stood for a moment in silence. The Fall breeze made its way through our hair and through the few inches that were between us. He gave me a half smile and took a step forward. Amazingly, my feet mimicked his, and we began our stroll through the cool, brisk air to my house.

We walked in awkward silence for the first block with only the sound of my heels, which were really uncomfortable. I'd been wearing them for seven hours straight and my feet were killing me now.

"So, have you lived here long?" he asked.

"Uh, yeah. I was in third grade when we moved here. You?" That was a stupid question. Everyone knew he started Middleton High at the beginning of sophomore year and was from Oregon. Stupid.

He chuckled as if he were reading my mind.

"My dad got a job offer the summer before sophomore year. So, we just left Oregon and came here."

"Do you miss home?" Another stupid question. Of course he missed his hometown.

"Yeah, I do. But this place is amazing. Oregon was so...bland. It's fun here. Everyone gets so excited about Mardi Gras and football. And everyone's so friendly. I had to get used to giving people a hug and a kiss whenever we say hi and goodbye."

I giggled. "It grows on you. It becomes a natural reflex after a while."

"So, where did you move from?" he asked.

"Um...California. My mom switched jobs and said she wanted to get away from the busy life. I don't remember L.A. much, though."

Tristen suddenly grabbed my arm when I clearly didn't realize we were walking into a busy intersection. His touch was warm.

"I've been to L.A. It wasn't bad. I'm kind of a movie junkie, so Hollywood was pretty exciting."

Another plus. It was no secret that horror flicks were my favorite. Mom hated my obsession with blood and gore.

"What kind of movies do you like?" My stomach knotted in anticipation of his answer.

"Um, I like everything. Action, because, well...I'm a guy." He smiled. "And probably scary movies. They just don't make them like they used to."

"That's what I say!" My voice shot up a few more octaves than I wanted. I blushed. He looked over at me and smiled sweetly. "I mean, horror movies are great," I said, lowering my tone.

"What's your favorite?" he asked.

"Uh...that's tough. I would have to say, the original *Texas Chainsaw Massacre.*"

"You have to admit, the remake was pretty good. Jessica Biel was very persuasive...and hot," he stated.

"Of course! I'm surprised any guy could even pay attention to the actual movie while she's running around in a wet, white T-shirt and tight jeans," I teased.

"Oh, so you noticed, too?"

I laughed before stopping abruptly. Tristen had walked a few steps ahead before he noticed I wasn't beside him anymore. He turned around. "Grace?"

I looked around and sucked in the air through my nose. I wasn't quite sure, but I could suddenly smell something familiar. Smokey and sweet aromas filled my lungs, and my stomach began to growl. I glanced at Tristen and realized he was patiently waiting for me to say something.

"Are you okay?" he asked.

"Yeah. Sorry. I just...I just remembered something I had to do for homework." I decided not to tell him the truth. I wasn't even sure what the truth was, anyway.

We were a block away from my house when my stomach began to feel like it was eating itself. The smell got stronger with every step we took, and I had to struggle to resist the urge to run until I found the source of it. Tristen didn't say another word. We walked in silence until we reached my house.

When I opened the door, the smell slapped me across my face. Tristen followed and quietly shut the door behind him.

"Mom!" I called out.

"In the kitchen, dear!"

I walked into the kitchen. My jaw dropped and my stomach flipped.

"Hi, Gracie. I made some snacks for your tutoring session. I'm sure you must be hungry." She quickly came to kiss my cheek and returned to her task of bringing dishes full of food to the table. I looked over at Tristen and his eyes popped open.

"Wow!"

My face flushed. "Uh, Mom, this is more like dinner...for a family of ten," I stated.

"Oh, Gracie. It's fine. Come. Sit and eat." She pulled out two chairs at the kitchen table and looked over to us. Tristen immediately made his way over. "And you must be Tristen," she said with a hint of sour. I wasn't sure if Tristen caught it, but I did.

"Yes, ma'am. Very nice to meet you." He quickly kissed her on the cheek before taking a seat. I could tell he was still not used to kissing total strangers.

My mom gave him a slight smile then gazed over to me. "Are you going to sit, Grace?"

I stood there, not sure of what I was supposed to do. My stomach was tearing my insides open as the seconds ticked by with the sight and smell of all the food. Tristen would be absolutely disgusted if he knew that I could eat every last bit of food on this table—and still have room for dessert. Oh, but it smelled so good.

Plates were filled with mini roast beef and turkey sandwiches, fried chicken tenders, tiny meatballs, stuffed mushrooms, and—oh God—my favorite, bacon-grits fritters. It was an all-you-could-eat buffet of deliciousness.

"Honey, you should really sit and get started on studying," Mom insisted. "You don't want to be working all night long."

I bit my bottom lip.

THE INVITATION

I FINALLY MADE THE decision to sit down, narrowing my eyes at my mother. Why would she do this to me? I couldn't shake the feeling of sabotage.

Tristen looked at me and smiled, clearly oblivious to what I was thinking, but completely in awe of my mother's southern hospitality.

"Okay, you kids get started on your work while I fix your plates. Tristen, what would you like to drink?" Mom asked as she walked over to the fridge.

"I'll take water, please." He was so polite.

"I'll take my usual, Mom. Oh, hey," I said to Tristen. "You should try my mom's famous pomegranate juice."

"Oh, darn! I only have enough for one glass," she said immediately as she poured the last drop into a glass. I stared at her face, confused. I could have sworn she had said she made a fresh pitcher last night.

"Well, you can have mine," I said to Tristen.

His brows furrowed. "No, you love it. You should have it." He smiled wide, showing his gloriously white teeth.

I blushed and glanced at my mom, who had a smile on her face as well. Maybe she actually liked him.

A pain shot across my stomach and I winced. I looked over at the food and began telling myself that I could do this. I could eat a normal amount of food. I didn't understand why I felt so unbelievably hungry over the past few days, but I forced myself to push those thoughts out of my head. I had to focus on keeping my secret from Tristen. At least for now. There was no way that a girl who could eat pounds of food in one sitting was at all attractive.

"Here you go, kids," Mom said while setting our glasses on the table. She then took our plates and began filling them with a sample from every dish. My serving seemed noticeably larger than Tristen's. Hopefully, he wouldn't notice.

"Here, you can try some juice. I promise that you'll love it," I said, reaching over to hand Tristen my glass. But before Tristen could grab hold of it, Mom fell into my arm and the glass slipped out of my hands. It smashed onto the kitchen floor—sweet, sweet pomegranate juice splattering all over the place.

"Oh...oh my God...Gracie! I'm so sorry!"

"Are you okay, Ms. Shelley?" Tristen asked, reaching out a hand to keep her steady. I couldn't help the grin slowly sweeping across my face for Tristen's concern.

"Yes. Thank you, Tristen. My foot must have caught the leg of the chair. I'm okay." She stood up, seeming a bit embarrassed for her clumsiness. Mom was never usually clumsy. She was always very poised and well-coordinated. I have never known my mother to clumsily miss her footing or anything even close.

"I'm so sorry, Gracie. I'll make some more tonight. Let me just clean this up and you two can continue on with your studying. Eat up." She grabbed a kitchen towel as we took out our books and notepads.

Tristen began eating some of what was on his plate. I, on the other hand, was fighting the urge to sneak my plate off into the bathroom to swallow everything whole. My stomach began to cave inward, and I knew it was only a matter of time before the room would start spinning and I would feel queasy.

I watched as Tristen casually grabbed a chicken tender and took a bite while he thumbed through his textbook, searching for the chapter we were supposed to study. I opened my textbook and mimicked his casualness. The salty and delicious fried creation melted into my taste buds, and I briefly closed my eyes in pure satisfaction. I focused on chewing instead of swallowing it whole—that was until my stomach felt like it reached into my throat and pulled it down. I peeked over at Tristen, who was now reading his notes.

I could do this.

Mom finished cleaning up the horrible death of my favorite juice and left the room. I swallowed hard, thinking of something clever to say to Tristen.

"So, what did you guys do today in class?" He beat me to it. Thank God.

"Oh, we just went over some of the stuff from earlier in the week. So...where were you today?" I asked. A little forthcoming, but I deserved to know, considering how he tortured me all day long.

He was in the middle of chewing his food and gave a throaty chuckle as if to let me know he was sorry he couldn't answer right away. I studied his jawline. It was strong and softly curved into his chin.

He swallowed and smiled. "Sorry. Uh...I had to go to a doctor's appointment," he said, rubbing the back of his neck.

"Oh. Are you okay?" I asked, genuinely hoping there wasn't anything wrong.

"Yeah, I'm fine. It wasn't my appointment."

I suddenly realized who it was for when I put two and two together, remembering that Sonny was not at school today, either.

"Oh. Well...good," I said, trying hard not to sound disappointed. Of course he would go support his girlfriend at the doctor's.

There was a moment of silence. I grabbed my notes out of my bag to begin our study session. Between trying to focus on not swooning over him the entire time we were sitting there and trying not to stuff my face with every last morsel on the table, the last thing I wanted to talk about was Sonny and her ailments.

Picturing her with some horribly disgusting disease did brighten me up a bit.

"Mind if I look over your notes?" he asked.

"Sure, go ahead. I'll look over yours to see what you're missing."

Tristen scooted his chair closer to mine and my pulse quickened. We were now only a few inches apart, and I could smell his sharp, clean cologne. It smelled like heaven.

We compared notes, and I began to explain the definite integral. This was a cakewalk for me, but there was something about watching him concentrate on learning that made my heart race. He seemed so lost but was listening carefully as I slowly explicated the problems in a simpler fashion. His eyebrows came together when he was confused, but his face lit up like a Christmas tree when he finally understood the concept. It was satisfying and sweet, which helped push out most of my thoughts about the food that was tempting my every desire.

My stomach was still screaming at me to eat more, but it seemed for now that my sensibly small bites were satisfying it.

A few hours went by, and we continued on our quest to get Tristen a perfect score on our upcoming test. Mom came in and out of the kitchen from time to time, peering over in our direction and giving us a smile. I knew better and figured she was checking to make sure we weren't making out. Or making sure that Tristen's hands weren't down my shirt.

Then, his phone rang. He pulled it out of his pocket and glanced at it before silencing the sound. I knew who it was.

"Do you need to go?" I asked, praying that he would say no.

"Oh, no. It's nothing." He shook his head and looked back down at his book. I wasn't quite sure why he refused to even say Sonny's name. It's not like I didn't know she was his girlfriend. But whatever the reason, I was grateful for it.

While we wrapped things up, Tristen briefly called his mom to let her know we were finished and that he was ready to be picked up. We sat in the living room and waited.

"Halloween is coming up soon," he announced. That statement alone gave me butterflies.

Halloween was my favorite time of the year. It boggled my mind to think that some people actually didn't celebrate Halloween. How could you not? Not that I sat at home and held séances, but it was an exciting holiday for me. People were allowed to be whoever they wanted to be. Children scurried from door to door collecting one of the most important things in their little lives—candy. And it was free!

People made plans to attend Halloween parties, spend time with their children trick-or-treating, roam the streets and work together to randomly scare others who walked by, and some even opted to just sit home with friends and family to watch gory, scary movies all night, which is what Phoebe and I did every single year to celebrate. In my opinion, blood, gore, and ax murderers were thrilling. And with the Fall breeze in the air, the leaves turning colors, and the moon lighting up the darkness in the night, it was better than Christmas, if you asked me.

"I know," I said with a stupid grin. "It's my favorite."

Tristen smiled wide and laughed. I wasn't sure if he was laughing at me. If he was, my ridiculous grin had something to do with it.

"Do you have plans?" he asked.

"Phoebe and I usually go haunted house hopping. Then we come home and watch horror movies until the sun comes up. It's sort of a tradition," I explained, suddenly feeling embarrassed. I realized that in Tristen's world, he probably attended parties all night long with the cool kids. And Sonny.

"That actually sounds like fun. We normally go to a party. It's getting kind of boring now. It's always the same people, getting drunk and sitting around. I haven't been to a haunted house since I was a kid."

"Really?" I asked, surprised. He had been deprived.

"Yeah. I mean, we always end up going to the same places. And no one ever dresses up anymore. Who wouldn't want to be someone different for a night?"

Did he just read my mind?

"Well, you can come hang out with us." The words were out of my mouth before I could stop them.

Was I insane? We had one study date, and now I was asking him to ditch his friends, his clique, his *girlfriend* to hang out with me and a girl he barely knew. He barely even knew me! And this wasn't even a date! Oh my God.

He raised his eyebrows and smiled. As he opened his mouth to say something, the sound of a car horn interrupted him. I slumped into the couch, mentally running outside and smashing that car into pieces.

"That's my mom. So, thanks for helping me. I needed this more than you know."

"Oh, I know." I smiled. "You would have needed a miracle to pass that test."

We stood up and headed toward the front door.

"Thanks for the vote of confidence." He chuckled.

I opened the door and he stopped to face me in the doorway. "Hey, it's okay. Mrs. Turner is tough," I said, attempting to soothe his ego.

"No, really. Thanks, Grace."

I felt the heat flush my face and ears, hoping it wouldn't show. "You're welcome."

He smiled and leaned in to give me a hug. My body froze, struggling to keep my composure. My legs could turn into jelly at any minute and I could fall to my knees. I hugged him back and took one big whiff of his scent.

He pulled away too soon and walked down the porch steps as I slowly close the door. Before I could shut it all the way, he yelled out my name.

"Hey, Grace!"

I opened the door. The butterflies in my stomach were having a party.

"You look beautiful today!"

I thought my heart had just fallen out of my butt.

He smiled wide, flashing his flawless teeth, and turned around to disappear into his mother's car. I watched them drive down the street and turn at the corner. When I closed the door, I fell back into it, letting every moment of the day sink into my mind—chuckling at the cliché movie moment I was having. Sure, he tortured me today. Sure, my mother tried to sabotage my date for some reason. Sure, I fought the battle between food and my stomach. And yes, I made a complete fool out of myself for pretty much asking him out. But I didn't care. The only thing that mattered to me was that he reacted. He reacted, and it was the reaction that I wanted. The reaction that proved he thought about me more than just a study buddy. I wasn't sure what it meant yet, but it meant something.

With that mission accomplished, my next mission was to confront my mother.

My stomach made a loud gurgle and I looked down at it.

Okay, food first. Then Mom.

THE TEST

I PEELED MYSELF AWAY from the front door and from thoughts of Tristen's sweet smile, and then headed toward the kitchen. All of the plates were still pretty much full. During our study session, I had managed to ingest enough food to hold me over, without convincing Tristen that I was some kind of freak. I had paced myself and daintily picked the smallest pieces on the plate. It was tough, but I managed. Now I was starving again, and I needed some food desperately.

I sat down at the dinner table, and without any thought, dug into every dish. The food was cold and dry by now, but I could still taste the delicious herbs and spices. Before I knew it, everything was gone, and yet I wanted more.

"Still hungry, Gracie?" Mom walked into the kitchen as if to have read my mind.

I glanced at her—still pissed from her behavior this afternoon—nodded and looked away.

She walked over to the refrigerator, and before she could pull out the dish covered in aluminum foil, I could smell the roast.

"I knew you would want more." She uncovered the container and a whiff of tender meat whipped around my head.

I needed it.

"Mom, you can just bring that over here. I don't mind it cold," I said, trying not to sound anxious.

Her brow knitted in confusion. She stared at me for a moment before walking over to the silverware drawer. She pulled out a fork and brought the dish over to the table. I watched every movement, every step she took, anticipating the moment I could savor the glorious pot roast. She set it down in front of me. Not able to hold off any longer, I dug into the meat.

Without a word, she left the room and headed upstairs. Was she mad at me? Whatever. I didn't really care. Food was more important. But I knew I needed to finish up quickly and go have a talk with her.

When I finished, which was all too soon, I prepared my speech and headed upstairs to her bedroom. I needed to know why she tried to sabotage my study date. Why would she purposely try to embarrass me in front of Tristen? Maybe she was unaware of my sudden uncontrollable yearning for food, but how could she forget the episode just the night before? And about that...I needed to ask her what was wrong with me. She was a doctor; she should at least have some idea as to why I had been feeling...different lately.

And what about the pomegranate juice? I knew she said she made a fresh batch last night. How could it have all been gone? I had never seen her drink it before. As a matter of fact, I could remember her saying it was too sweet for her and that she preferred something less sugary.

I made my way to her bedroom and knocked on the door. When she didn't answer, I slowly opened the door into darkness. She was asleep. Great.

I closed the door quietly and headed into my bedroom, making mental notes of all of my questions. I would just have to ask her in the morning.

The following day, I awoke to the smell of bacon, sausage, and the usual aromas of a breakfast feast. Before I knew it, I was throwing the covers off of me and heading down the stairs. I was starved.

I entered the kitchen to find dishes full of my much-loved breakfast items...and a note. I grabbed a piece of bacon and read the note.

Gracie,

I had to head out early to work. As you can see, breakfast is made, and lunch is already in your bag for school. I will see you this afternoon. Please be sure to eat your meals today.

I love you.

Mom

Well, she certainly didn't have to worry about me eating breakfast.

Phoebe smacked me on the arm when I met her in our usual spot for our walk to school.

"Why didn't you call me last night after your date?" she yelled.

"Ouch!"

"Sorry," she apologized.

"Phoebe! I was just tired."

"So, did you guys...you know..." She wiggled her eyebrows up and down.

It was my turn to smack her on the arm. "No! It wasn't like that."

"Ouch!" She smiled and smacked me again. "So, what was it like?"

I rubbed my arm once more and smiled back. My heart began racing at the memory of sitting so close to Tristen.

"We just studied."

"That's it?" Phoebe asked, clearly disappointed. In her mind, Tristen should have walked into the house, thrown me on the kitchen table, and had his way with me. Although that scenario didn't sound too bad, my version would have included food. Maybe he would be feeding it to me.

I smiled dreamily at that thought.

"And you're okay with that?"

"Okay with what?" I asked. I was still thinking about food and Tristen...together.

"G, you had the hottest guy in school, the guy that you have been daydreaming about for, like...ever, at your house, and you didn't make a move?" This was preposterous to Phoebe. She was not some easy chick, but she would have at least made it to first base with him.

"Well, Phoebe, not all of us have the guts that you do. I couldn't just make out with him right there in my kitchen, not with my mother keeping an eye on us."

"Oh, right. Mom was there. So, was there at least some flirting going on?" She sounded defeated but hopeful.

"You could say that." I grinned. "He told me I was beautiful."

Phoebe shoved me. "Get out!"

I wanted to punch her for hitting the same arm for the third time, but I couldn't keep from giggling like the teenager that I was. Tristen Miles thought I was beautiful.

"So, are you guys gonna hang out again?"

"He asked me about Halloween."

"Is he coming with us?" She could not contain herself any longer.

"Well, I sort of asked him to. I'm sorry, Phoebe. I know it's normally just me and you. It just kind of came out. He probably won't even—"

"No! It's perfect. Eric wants to come hang out with us, too. It'll be a double date!"

A double date. A date. A real date with Tristen. This concept sent the butterflies in my belly on a rampage, and I held on to that thought as we approached our day at school.

The day dragged on, as usual, but I couldn't help the sappy grin across my face. I didn't see Tristen until Calculus. We walked through the door almost at the same time. When we were nearly touching each other, he leaned in and whispered into my ear, "Good luck." The smell of his minty breath cooled my senses and the feel of it sent tingles down my spine. Those two words flowed through me like silk as I fought the urge to fall into his arms.

"Good luck," was all I could manage to respond.

I was happy. I knew Tristen was going to ace this test and it was because of me. I was going to save him from failing and from getting kicked off the swim team. It would be because of my weird math genius that he'd be in a great mood today.

After roll call and about fifteen minutes of answering lingering questions students had regarding the material, Mrs. Turner handed out our tests and started the clock. This test was a piece of cake, and I knew I could pass it with my eyes closed. I was the top in our class, and I knew everyone hated how math came so easily to me. I wondered why I never started tutoring sessions for students. It would have been a great way to make some cash on the side.

Halfway through completing the test, a sharp pain shot across my belly. My reflexes forced me to clench onto my stomach, and I winced. Julie, the cute little redhead who sat next to me, looked over in my direction and noticed my pained expression.

"Grace," she whispered. "You okay?"

I turned to her, nodded, and glanced back down at my paper. I was getting the hunger pains again.

I looked up at the clock. Only thirty more minutes until lunch. Wrapping an arm around my belly, I tried to force myself to only think about the test. The definite integral. I just explained this to Tristen yesterday, this was simple.

But as I prepared to work out the equations in my mind, I...I couldn't. I couldn't figure it out. I couldn't remember how to do the problems, or even what the definite integral meant. It was like my mind got confused, unable to understand. And as if that weren't bad enough, the numbers and letters began to intertwine into one, and I could no longer make out what it said. I scanned the rest of the classroom, watching everyone else struggle to answer the questions. But not for the same reasons.

The room began spinning. I closed my eyes, took a deep breath, and looked back down at the test. It didn't help. The pain worsened until I was hunched over. I squinted my eyes, trying hard to focus. My head began to throb, and my eyesight blurred. I caught a glimpse of my bookbag on the floor from the corner of my eye. And then, the faint aroma of roast beef and turkey made its way to my nose. It was as if I had suddenly developed x-ray vision—as if I could see straight through my bag. I could see the sandwich and the rest of my lunch inside a paper bag, waiting to be eaten. My mouth watered, but I forced myself to return my focus to the test.

"Five-minute warning," Mrs. Turner said from her desk. My head shot up. How did twenty-five minutes already fly by? I was only halfway done!

I glanced over at Tristen. He looked pretty confident. I wasn't sure if that made me feel better or worse.

Okay, I can do this, I told myself.

I set my elbows down on the desk and ran my fingers through my hair. Something felt weird. I pulled my hands back down and gasped.

A chunk of my hair fell in my palm. I quickly tightened my hand into a fist to hide it. I looked around to see if anyone else had noticed. I had to get out of the classroom.

I grabbed my bag and my test and made my way to Mrs. Turner's desk.

"I'm sorry, Mrs. Turner. I have to go." My voice was hoarse.

"Grace, are you okay?"

I ignored her and headed to the door. The bell rang and hurt my ears. And right as I reached to turn the knob, darkness took over me.

THE THREAT

MY EYES FLUTTERED OPEN. The smell of alcohol burned my nose.

"There you go. Wake up for me, Grace." A soft female voice spoke into my left ear. I peered at Nurse Nancy sitting next to me, waving something around my nose. I didn't want to be rude, but the smell was about to make me gag. I gently pushed her arm away and she got the hint.

"How are you feeling, dear?"

Nurse Nancy was a stout woman. She was older and had a quality about her—like she was once very beautiful, but the years had not been kind to her. She knew her work well and seemed to have been doing it for a long time. She knew when a student was faking an illness and would kick them out of her office in a heartbeat. But if they really were ill, she was kind and sweet and very nurturing.

I stared up at the ceiling for a moment before attempting to sit up. I had to pull myself together. There was a slight pain in my stomach, but not quite as bad as before. My hands shot up to my head, feeling around to make sure my hair was all still there. To my relief, it was.

"W-what happened?" I could barely speak. The sterile paper underneath me crunched as I sat up.

"You fainted," Nurse Nancy said, jotting something down on the documents in front of her. "Do you faint often? Did you recently fall, injuring your head? Do you feel nauseous at all?"

I shook my head no to all of her questions, trying hard not to move too much. It was still throbbing, but not too bad.

"Did you eat breakfast this morning?"

"Yes," I mumbled.

"Well, sometimes if we're really hungry and don't eat, or if we don't eat enough, we can begin to feel bad or queasy or even faint. I don't see any other signs that point to this being something serious. Maybe you just didn't eat enough this morning. I had an IV hooked up to you for a little bit while you were out, just to get some fluids in you."

"Did you call my...mom?" I asked. I knew Mom would freak out if she wasn't made aware of something like this happening to me.

"We did call your mother. She's actually in the front office getting you checked out for the day. You should go home and get some rest. Get a good meal or two in. But take it easy for the rest of the day. I don't think you have a concussion, but just in case. I'm going to update your mom in a minute and recommend making a doctor's appointment, just to make sure your fainting spell isn't anything more serious."

She closed what I assumed to be my file and took my vitals before heading toward the door.

"I'm going to let your mom know you're awake."

I nodded and she left the room.

Well, this was wonderful. I didn't finish my test. This would be the first time in the history of my schooling that I wasn't able to finish a test and possibly flunked it. I had never made a mark lower than a B in my life! And in math! Out of all—

Oh. My. God. I passed out? In class? In front of Tristen?

I dropped my head into my hands and fought the urge to cry. I couldn't decide what was worse—falling and revealing my holey granny panties to the entire school a few years ago or fainting in front of Tristen. I pictured myself passing out, hitting the ground hard, arms and legs completely sprawled out with my mouth wide open, tongue hanging out, and drool oozing onto the floor.

Yeah. I'd guess both instances were equally mortifying.

There was a knock on the door of the small, hospital-like room. Great. I had to deal with my mother. For some reason, I knew she would blame me for what happened. I was sure she thought that I didn't eat enough breakfast. The truth was, I ate it all...and then some. I actually didn't feel full after my bacon, sausage, pancakes, hash browns, eggs, and pigs in a blanket, so I ate a dish of leftover pasta.

Before I could get out of the cot to open the door, it swung open. "Grace?"

I paused, not quiet believing who stood in the doorway.

"Sonny?"

She smiled and walked in, shutting the door behind her. I wasn't sure if I was frightened or nervous. This couldn't be good.

"Hi, Grace," she said in a soft, almost too-kind voice.

I pulled my eyebrows together, trying to understand why she was in here.

She sashayed over to the chair next to the cot. I watched her intently, expecting her to pull out a shank to attack me. I braced myself.

"How are you feeling?" Her question almost sounded genuine, which confused me even more.

I was silent, hesitant to answer her. Finally, I said, "Better."

"Good. You had us all worried."

Us? Who was she talking about? I glanced over at the door, planning a quick escape in my head. There was no way she was being serious. She had to have a shank hidden somewhere.

"It's okay, silly." She smiled, sensing my hesitation. "I just came to see if you were feeling well."

I was considering a thank you but couldn't find those words. She sat back in the chair and began looking around on Nurse Nancy's desk. She found a nail file and proceeded to file her nails. Was this some kind of joke?

"When I heard that you passed out in class, I was really concerned...for a few reasons. For one, I worried you might have hurt your head."

She giggled and shook her head. I knew that wasn't true.

"Two, I thought I might have missed the free show you were giving everyone." Her eyes lowered down to my legs. "But then I saw that you were wearing jeans, not a skirt. So...I didn't miss much."

I knew this was going to get ugly. I grabbed onto the cot tightly, resisting the urge to swing.

She continued filing. "And three, I thought I would miss my chance to ask you how last night went." She looked up from her nails and stared straight into my eyes. I let go of the cot, feeling defeated.

Crap. Of course she knew about last night. I was so caught up in the sweet moments Tristen and I shared that I didn't even think twice about seeing Sonny the next day in school.

"So, how did it go?" She leaned over in the chair as if awaiting the juiciest gossip she had ever heard.

I took a deep breath, trying to somehow conjure up a lie. I could tell her that it didn't happen. But that wouldn't make sense. She already knew it was happening and Tristen probably told her. It seemed like my only option here was to be honest.

"It went fine. We studied," I said, shrugging my shoulders. It was the truth, anyway. We did study.

"Right." She nodded slowly. "You helped him for his test today. I tried to call him, but he wouldn't answer, which is weird because he always answers the phone for me. Why do you think he didn't answer?"

I knew that she did try calling and he had silenced her call. I asked myself the same question when I saw him do it.

This impromptu meeting with Sonny was getting annoying.

"Sonny, I...I honestly don't know," I said. I made sure to sound irritated so she would get the hint.

She sat back in her chair and stared at me. There was a moment of silence, and I started to wonder when the hell she would get to her point.

She finally spoke. "Okay, Grace. Listen." Her voice was low. "I'm only going to tell you this one time, and one time only. Tristen doesn't need your help. He will never need your help. I know you have this... crush...on my boyfriend. If you think for one second that you have any chance in hell of somehow stealing him from me or trying to pry into our relationship, you are sadly mistaken. He is mine. He has always been mine."

She stood up from her chair and took a step toward me. I sat up firm, gripping onto the cot again. She lifted her perfectly manicured finger and pointed it in my face.

"Playing the damsel in distress and passing out in front of him is not going to win him over. If you don't back off, I promise you I'll make your life hell. Besides, he's way out of your league."

She turned on her heel and whipped her strawberry blonde hair around before sashaying back out of the door. I exhaled a deep breath and slumped into the cot. Why didn't I just grab her hair when she turned around and pulled it out of her skull? She was threatening me. And I wasn't sure if my feelings were of fright, defeat, or determination.

After Mom checked me out of school, we walked over to the car in silence. I wasn't sure if she was upset, but she certainly didn't seem happy. As we secured our seatbelts and Mom started the car, I decided to find out.

"Mom, are you upset with me?"

"No, Grace. I'm not," she said without expression. "I just have a lot on my mind. How are you feeling?"

"Better. I just wanna go home and lie down." I truly felt drained.

"Not before you get some food in you."

I decided this was the moment to bring up what happened last night.

"Mom, I wanted to ask you about last night. Why did you make all that food for Tristen and me?"

"What do you mean, Gracie?" She chuckled. "I was being a good mother, providing a meal for my daughter and her friend. Is that a bad thing?"

"No, it's not. You just know how I've been feeling lately about... eating. And with what happened the night before, I just felt like you were trying to purposely humiliate me."

"Humiliate you? Why would I want to do that?"

We pulled up to the house and made our way inside. Mom headed straight for the kitchen to begin cooking for me. I followed and sat at the kitchen table.

"Well, dear?" she asked as she grabbed ingredients out of the fridge.

"I don't know. I was wondering the same thing. I mean, I know you said you didn't agree with Tristen and me hanging out. I just thought that—"

"Grace, I was trying to give you advice about the situation."

I felt annoyed. "Yeah, but you don't agree with me hanging out with him."

"You're right, I don't." She stopped prepping and stared at me for a moment. "I'm just trying to protect you, Gracie."

I sighed. "Protect me from what, Mom? From someone that I like, who likes me back?"

"He likes you, too? Are you sure?"

I looked away. "Well, I'm pretty sure..."

"Then let him come to you. Do not pursue him. If you get into the middle of his relationship, then it won't end well."

This piece of information seemed pretty valuable. In some ways—most ways—she was right. I shouldn't come between Tristen and Sonny. He could break up with her, bring her down gently, and then come to me. However, because of our lovely encounter and her incredibly bitchy I'm-better-than-you attitude, I was not bowing down so easily.

"So, about the night before last. What do you think that was about?" I asked casually.

"What about it?" she shot back immediately. Was she serious?

"Um...by the way I looked and felt, I'm assuming that something was wrong with me. Not to mention all of the food I devoured in, like, thirteen seconds."

"Oh, honey. I'm not worried. You're seventeen. Your body is evolving. You're going through hormonal changes right now. You'll be fine." She didn't seem at all worried. This made me feel a bit better.

"Okay, I guess. I just haven't been feeling...myself lately."

She stopped and peered over at me. Now she seemed concerned. "Well, what have you been feeling?" she asked.

"I don't know. Just tired, I guess. I've been really, really hungry all the time. When I eat, I feel much better. But when I'm hungry, my body feels...beaten up or something. I feel like I need to eat all the time. And I'm just so hungry." I grabbed my stomach, suddenly feeling starved.

I could tell she was worried, but there seemed to be an emotion in her eyes that I couldn't quite figure out. Sadness?

She turned back to the stove and resumed cooking. "Well, you're fine, Gracie. I'm sure of it," she said over her shoulder.

I watched her as she continued on with her chef duties.

My mother was quite a woman. With a curvy, statuesque figure and wavy, dark shoulder-length hair, she was a looker. I had witnessed, with my own two eyes, men of all ages checking her out when we had gone to the supermarket.

She carried herself with class, and she was very polite and proper. But something told me deep down that Mom had a crazy side to her. I was almost positive that in her younger years, she was wild. Maybe even wilder than Phoebe.

But besides her looks and personality, my mother was a very educated woman. She was top in her class through high school and medical school. She became a neurosurgeon and was awarded Doctor of the Year a few years before I was born. Apparently, a few years *after* I was born, she got into some kind of accident and lost her index finger. It got caught in a fence, or something like that? I wasn't too sure.

Anyway, considering her job entailed having to operate on tiny nerves, it was important for her to be able to hold medical equipment properly. So, she had to resign. A couple of years later, a friend of a friend needed an assistant here in New Orleans, so my mom decided to take the job.

Working as an assistant to a forensic pathologist was a far cry from being one of the best neurosurgeons in the state of California.

It was completely different working with deceased people than on a person who was actually alive. But she was able to stay close to her medical roots and she seemed pretty content.

She didn't really like to talk about her time as a surgeon. She had told me little things here and there, and I could tell by her glow whenever she talked about it that she had really enjoyed it. I still felt like she might have been destined to be a chef, though. Maybe it was her attention to detail and her training as a neurosurgeon to be incredibly meticulous. Either way, cooking was certainly something she did well.

With all of her capabilities and her looks, I often wondered why she had never remarried. I was sure she could have any man she wanted.

And if she claimed that I was okay, I believed her.

THE BEEF

AFTER A PRE-DINNER SNACK of chicken pot pie, the main course soon followed. Mom and I sat silently at the dinner table.

After dinner, I headed upstairs with a belly full of meatloaf, salad, mashed potatoes, bacon-wrapped asparagus, cranberry sauce, and corned beef hash to get some homework done. Mom informed me that Mrs. Turner was going to allow me to retake the test on Monday. When I opened my textbook to begin studying, I realized it was Friday and I had all weekend to study up. Silly me.

I plopped on the bed and booted up my laptop. It was time to be nosy. I was aware that it was Friday night and being home poking around on Facebook was not the cool thing to do, but whatever. The only person I really wanted to hang out with was Phoebe, but of course, she was too busy trying to woo Eric.

As soon as I logged into my profile, there was a message in my inbox. My heart skipped a beat. Could it be Tristen? Was he worried about me? I didn't know Tristen as well as I was hoping to get to know him just yet, but I was sure that he was as compassionate as they come. I mean, he skipped school to accompany his girlfriend to the doctor. I could just see her pouting to get what she wanted. Puppy-dog eyes that probably soon glowered more and more as she looked at him; bottom lip sulking just enough for him to finally give in. But I did still wonder what the appointment was for. A case of something really embarrassing, I hoped.

I clicked on the inbox as my heart skipped several more beats. A message from...Sonny? Oh, this should be good.

There was a link to a picture. I opened the link, curiosity coursing through me.

It loaded, and lo and behold, a picture of her and Tristen, kissing. Underneath it, the caption read:

You will never have this.

XOXO, Sonny.

I melted into my headboard and stared at the picture. I've got to say, it was a sweet photo. They were facing each other. Her hair flowy and beautiful. Her ruby lips puckered and made contact with his. He smiled through their kiss. It was charming, and even though it hurt to see him really happy, I imagined it was me.

So, this was how she wanted to play the game. Our little rendezvous in the nurse's office was frightening, to say the least, simply because I was worried for my safety, but it also showed just how insecure she was about their relationship. If she didn't feel threatened by me, why would she have wasted her time, anyway?

If she wanted a war, she was going to get one. And I was ready to win it. I may be a girl with simple tastes who played video games and enjoyed watching B-rated slasher movies rather than plotting revenge on innocent people, but this was a special circumstance. Sonny was not so innocent. She was mean to anyone who didn't fit into her world. I didn't feel so bad about possibly breaking up her and Tristen's relationship. Especially not if he was showing interest in me. Besides, I had better hair than she did.

Right as I was about to shut down my computer, an instant message pinged. It was Tristen.

Tristen Miles: *Hi.*

Grace Shelley: *Hey.*

Tristen Miles: *How are you feeling? I was worried about you.*

My heart jumped. He was worried?

Grace Shelley: *Much better.*

Tristen Miles: *Good.*

Okay. Small talk. I could do this.

Grace Shelley: *Did you do well on your test?*

Tristen Miles: *I did better than well. I'm pretty sure I aced it, thanks to you :)*

Grace Shelley: *Me...not so much. Mrs. Turner is letting me retake it, though.*

Tristen Miles: *I would hope so! If not, I would have to have a talk with her.*

Standing up for me? I liked it.

Grace Shelley: *Lol! So, did I miss much from the rest of the day?*

Tristen Miles: *Not really. I carried you to the nurse's office and I wanted to stay, but I had to meet up with Coach.*

He what?! I couldn't breathe. He carried me to the office? I stared at his words, double checking to see if I read them correctly.

Tristen Miles: *Grace?*

Grace Shelley: *So, you carried me?*

Tristen Miles: *Well, yeah. As soon as you fell, I ran over to you. I was worried you'd hit your head. Mrs. Turner and everyone else were kind of shocked that you had just passed out in front of the class and I didn't want you just lying there. I didn't know what was wrong.*

Embarrassment washed over me.

Grace Shelley: *Oh...I just didn't eat enough this morning.*

Tristen Miles: *Well, thank God it wasn't anything more serious. With your mom's cooking skills, I'm sure you were very satisfied when you got home.*

More than he knew. My stomach growled.

Grace Shelley: *I'm sure if Sonny saw you carrying me, she would not have been happy.*

Ugh...why did I just type that?

Tristen Miles: *She did see us. Everyone did. The bell had just rung.*

Great. Everyone saw. And so did Sonny. That must have been what pushed her to confront me. This was my chance.

Grace Shelley: *So...have you thought more about Halloween? I mentioned it to Phoebe, and she said it would be cool for all of us to hang out. She wants to bring Eric too.*

Tristen Miles: *A double date?*

Oh, God. Coming on too strong, too soon. Not good.

Grace Shelley: *Um...well...it wouldn't be a double date...I mean, it would just be friends...hanging out.*

Tristen Miles: *Well, count me in.*

Wow. That was easier than I thought. My smile could not have gotten any wider. But it faded quickly when I felt an ache in my belly. Oh, please. Not now.

Grace Shelley: *Awesome. I'll let Phoebe know.*

Tristen Miles: *Cool. Well, I better get going. I have to go meet up with the team and kick some ass in bowling.*

Grace Shelley: *Okay. Have fun!*

Tristen Miles: *Thanks. I'm glad you're feeling better, Grace. I was really worried about you.*

Grace Shelley: *Well, I'm just sorry you had to carry my dead weight across campus.*

Tristen Miles: *Lol! Trust me, I was okay with that. See ya.*

I was too busy trying to find my breath to answer him back. My chest caved in, and before I could respond, he was offline. He took care of me, he was worried about me, and he didn't mind carrying me? I didn't want to make quick assumptions, simply because I truly was taking what my mother had said about being let down into consideration, but I was pretty positive that he was showing some interest. I knew not giving up would pay off. Making an ass out of myself in front of the whole class was certainly not done intentionally, but it did win me a few points.

A stabbing pain deep in my belly made me hunch over. I grabbed my stomach and grimaced. I needed food.

I rushed downstairs as fast as I could and headed toward the kitchen. I reached into the fridge and began pulling out leftovers. Suddenly, I turned my nose up in the air. Something caught my attention. A different smell. A smell that seemed familiar, but I wasn't quite sure.

It was pungent and appealing. Iron, maybe? Raw. Like raw meat. That was it!

I ignored the smell, continuing on with my quest to satisfy my hungry stomach. But the smell of raw meat overpowered everything. My mouth watered, and I wasn't sure if it was because of the leftovers or the meat.

I uncovered the dishes and dug in. My mother's food was so delicious, but I couldn't stop thinking about raw meat. Where was it coming from, anyway?

With a hunk of meatloaf in hand, I began sniffing around the kitchen, trying to pick up the scent. I stepped into the living room for a moment, just to make sure it wasn't radiating out of there. But it definitely smelled stronger in the kitchen. I searched around with my nose. Maybe Mom dropped a piece somewhere while she was cooking.

I sniffed the counter tops, the sink, the kitchen table, and even the floor. I went to the fridge. I could smell it a little stronger, but I didn't find any raw meat. I opened the freezer and the smell smothered my face. It was, without a doubt, in the freezer.

I investigated. The smell should have been nauseating, but it was actually quite appealing. My mouth continued to water as I stood in front of the freezer, taking in the bloody scent. I inspected, not completely sure of what I was looking for. The meat was packed in individual gallon bags. They were assorted, I assumed, by red meat, poultry, and game. My mother was the cook, I certainly wasn't. I hadn't a clue what the different meats looked like except that red meat was red.

There were times when I would try to look over Mom's shoulder to learn how she did things, but she always shooed me away. She'd say that one day she would teach me all she knew and that as long as I lived under her roof, I could count on her calling the shots in the kitchen. This was okay by me. I didn't believe I could ever be as amazing a cook as my mom.

Wait a minute. Was frozen meat even supposed to smell? I knew that there was a slight odor, but not as strong as when it wasn't frozen.

It was as if my mother brought a cow in here and chopped it up on the kitchen counter about five minutes ago.

The smell was... inviting. It swirled around me, and my stomach began to rumble.

What did raw meat even taste like?

I pulled out a bag of dark meat, which had a date written on it in my mother's handwriting. I turned the bag over and around to get a good look at it. I became curious.

I opened the bag and breathed the smell. My eyes rolled as I inhaled. Oh, it smelled heavenly. I couldn't hold back any longer. I reached in and slid my index finger over the frozen carcass. I knew I wouldn't be able to just grab a piece—it was frozen.

Instead, I licked my finger to see if I could get a taste. There was something, something that I could no longer resist. I brought the bag to my mouth and bit down. My lips wrapped around the meat and my mouth started to suck. It was surprisingly not as hard as I thought the frozen meat would be, and I could feel my teeth begin to sink in. I couldn't bite completely into it, but it was enough for me to get a nibble.

It was tantalizing. I closed my eyes in satisfaction and stood in front of the open freezer, holding the bag full of frozen meat to my mouth as if it were a hamburger.

"Grace?"

It took everything out of me to turn my head away from the succulent meat.

Mom stood in the doorway, confusion written all over her face. When she realized what I was doing, the color of her face changed to white.

"Grace! What are you doing?" she asked as she rushed over to me and attempted to pull the bag out of my hands. I threw my hand back, realizing what she was trying to do. She paused and gave me a puzzled look. I had never undermined my mother before.

"Grace, give it to me," she said sternly.

I shook my head no. I wasn't completely sure what I was feeling at that moment. All I knew was that this was mine.

She tried again to snatch the bag, reaching over my shoulder. I grabbed her wrist with my free hand and squeezed. We were face to face, and the look in her eyes resembled a mixture of pain, disconcertion, and confusion. I couldn't say anything. My mission was to protect this bag.

She tried to pull away, but I squeezed tighter. "Gracie, you're hurting me." She struggled to get out of my grip for a few moments until she realized she couldn't.

I didn't speak. I didn't move. My mind was completely void of any thoughts except what I was holding in my other hand.

Finally, when I glanced at the kitchen table and realized that my stomach was not completely satisfied, I let go of her and headed toward the food. All I wanted to do was eat and hold onto the bag. Mom stood still, looking dumbfounded about what just happened.

THE WOUND

AFTER ABOUT TEN MINUTES of cleaning every last crumb off the plates, I was finally full.

I sat at the table alone, staring at the dishes, and then at the bag. I suddenly felt the urge to vomit. Was I seriously sucking on a frozen, raw piece of beef?

I swallowed back the bile in my throat and began cleaning up the mess. I threw the frozen meat into the garbage, feeling ridiculous for what I was trying to do. How could I possibly think raw meat was delicious?

Well, there were people who ate raw meat all around the world. Or how about sushi? Everyone loved sushi and it was raw fish. Wanting to eat raw meat wasn't that bad, was it?

I walked out of the kitchen, shaking those thoughts out of my head and making an internal promise to never try that again—unless I wanted to die of food poisoning.

As I made my way upstairs, memories of my mother in the kitchen flooded back.

Oh my God. She was in the kitchen. And I grabbed her! I picked up the pace and headed to her bedroom to apologize. How could I have done that? I would never hurt my mother. Ever!

Her door was slightly open, and her bedroom light was off. As I slowly pushed the door to open wider, I could hear her whispering voice on the other side. I leaned my ear closer into the gap and slowed my breathing.

"...well, I'm not sure if I want to do that. I don't believe it would be the best thing for her."

Was she talking about me? Her voice was uneasy.

"I left California to shield her. To protect her. I left everything I knew. Megan has no idea where I am."

She sounded strained, and I could tell she was crying. My mother never cried. She was as guarded and unemotional as they came. And who was Megan? And to protect me from what?

"It's getting worse, Mark. I don't know how much longer I can do this."

Mark was Dr. Walker, the handsome doctor friend who came to visit the other day. I wondered if he and Mom were secretly involved romantically. But there seemed to be something more than that. Something involving me.

I leaned in closer.

"Well, we're going to have to figure something else out. Sending her to—"

My attempt to shift my weight to hear her better without making any noise failed, and my shoulder bumped the door instead. *Shit!* I paused, as did Mom. Then I slowly backed away from the door, praying that she wouldn't open it. I headed to my room down the hall, silently stepping and hoping the wooden floors wouldn't decide to be charmingly creaky tonight.

I got into my room safely and plopped down on the bed.

What was she about to say? Send me where? Why would my mom want to send me anywhere? To boarding school, maybe? Who does that anymore these days, anyway? It wasn't like I was a terrible teenager. I made good grades at school. I never got into trouble. If anything, I was an *abnormal* teenager. I didn't go out often. I did my homework every night. Things had been awkward lately, with my hormonal eating and making a fool out of myself in front of the whole school, but that wasn't it. Was it? I mean, I knew she didn't agree with my feelings for Tristen, but that was still not enough. If she was trying to shield me from ever being with a guy, well, that was just ridiculous.

And who was Megan?!

I woke up the next morning to a familiar sharp pain in my stomach and the smell of raw meat. My entire body ached. When I attempted to maneuver myself out of the sheets, my bones felt as though they needed WD-40.

I finally scraped myself out of bed, limping with every step I took toward the bathroom. God, I felt like shit! My stomach felt like it was touching my back, or like I haven't eaten in a month. Every inch of my skin hurt. My head pounded. I thought about skipping the bathroom and just heading straight to the refrigerator, but I needed to go.

After doing my business, I stood up to flush the toilet. I gasped when I looked down into it. The toilet bowl was filled with red! What the hell was wrong with my insides? It didn't hurt coming out.

I felt the urge to run to my mother but just couldn't find the strength. Instead, I stood in front of the sink with my eyes closed. I was so tired I could barely keep them open. I splashed some cold water on my face to wake myself up. After drying it, I pulled the towel away from my face and noticed a tiny bit of blood.

I shot my head up to look in the mirror. Aside from my limp hair, the deep, dark circles around my eyes, and the blotching on my face, my bottom lip was bleeding. I leaned in closer to get a better look. A piece of skin hung off my lip, almost like it was severely chapped. Just like anyone else would do, I pinched the piece of skin between my fingernails, pulling slowly to get rid of it. But as I pulled, my lip followed, and the tiny piece began to grow. I winced. Blood rushed to the surface, formulating into a tear drop. I wiped it away with the towel and attempted to pull the piece off again. This time, a larger piece of skin followed, and I realized that a chunk of my lip came with it.

I couldn't stop. It needed to come off. I pulled further, and the piece continued to travel down from my lip to my chin. Blood began rushing faster and faster, drops falling into the sink. I let go, leaving the piece free to hang down my face.

Surprisingly, it didn't hurt as much as it should have. I wasn't sure if it was because I was already feeling terrible or not.

I searched the top drawer of the sink cabinet for a pair of scissors. After finding a pair of nail clippers instead, I clipped the long piece of thick flesh. I threw it in the toilet and inspected my face in the mirror. Wasn't skin and a cut this deep supposed to be pink? My underlying skin seemed to have a brown tint. I glanced up at the light bulbs. It must have been the lighting.

I pressed the towel down over the wound to stop the bleeding. It wasn't bleeding as much as I thought it should be, either. Strange.

My stomach snarled at me, followed by a shooting pain. I had to eat. To be honest, I wasn't as interested in what was happening to my lip. I wasn't sure if it was something to be alarmed about, because the intoxicating smell of that raw meat in the garbage was more important.

My attempt to rush down the stairs to the kitchen was unsuccessful. Every step felt as though my bones were cracking into two. I glanced over at my mother's bedroom door, which was opened, but she didn't seem to be in there.

After finally reaching the bottom step, I looked over to the living room and all I could hear was the ticking of our grandfather clock. I peeked over to my left and the kitchen was empty. There was a note on the table.

Gracie,
I had to work this morning. Breakfast is in the fridge. I love you.
Mom

Well, at least she cooked some breakfast for me after what happened last night. I was sure that she'd be too pissed off.

I made my way to the fridge to retrieve my chow. The smell of bacon, eggs, toast, and all of the irresistible odors of a wholesome morning breakfast seeped into my lungs before I could even open the refrigerator door. As I reached out to open it, the smell of raw meat took over. I glanced at the garbage can. Was the meat still in there?

I walked over and slowly lifted the lid. The smell grew stronger, and I could feel my stomach turning. My heart began to race, and my breaths grew quicker. It was still there.

My eyes couldn't turn away. My mind told me to leave it alone. There was no way that I would allow myself to dig into the filthy garbage to grab a chunk of rotting beef. But my body began to shake, and an uncontrollable urge to have that chunk of beef in my mouth swept over me.

Without hesitation I reached in, grabbed the beef, and sunk my teeth in. It was warm. I hunched over the garbage can as I chewed and chewed. The meat was dry, with a taste I couldn't place. It was disgusting. Coppery, but it was so, so delicious...and familiar. I thought of nothing else but what I was putting into my mouth. Not even the fact that I was literally devouring a chunk of balmy, dry, rare-beyond-rare meat.

When I was done, I continued to lean forward over the garbage. I waited to vomit—even gagging a few times—but nothing came out. Should I make myself vomit?

What did I just eat? The honest truth was that it was so good, I didn't even care.

I straightened my body after a few minutes, still feeling hungry. Without another thought, I headed to the fridge to get my real breakfast. I sat at the table, grabbing handfuls out of the dishes to feed my belly. My body felt better and better with every bite I took, and once I was completely done, I was ready to start my day. I washed the dishes and headed upstairs to shower.

Before getting into the shower, I glanced into the mirror to assess my face. My eyes were big and bright, my hair was long, curly, and shining, and my lip was healed. I ran my index finger over where the wound had been. Nothing there. How could that be? Was I dreaming that my lip was bleeding? I must have been dreaming.

Confused, I hopped into the shower, deciding to—yet again— shrug off the awkwardness that was plaguing me on a daily basis.

My phone rang when I was putting on my clothes. It was Phoebe. "Hey, Phoebe."

"Hey, Grace. Whatcha doing?" she asked innocently.

"Nothing, just got out the shower. Aren't you working this morning?"

"Yeah, but it's slow. Come see me."

"I don't know. I have to study for the retake test on Monday, and Mr. Kincaid gave us a ton of homework in Civics." I sounded like such a geek.

"Oh, come on, Grace. You can meet Eric! His shift starts in an hour. Please? I need you right now."

"Why do you need me?" I giggled.

"Because I miss you, G," she said.

"You just saw me yesterday at school." I smiled. I enjoyed giving her a hard time.

"Well, I wanna see you agaaain," she whined.

Phoebe was so cute sometimes. "Fine, be there in an hour."

"Yay!"

I hung up the phone and finished getting dressed. Skinny jeans, *Chuck Taylors*, and a baby tee sounded good. I decided to continue my quest on gaining more self-esteem with some light makeup. Phoebe was right. I did feel much better when I put this stuff on my face. I needed more practice, though.

With two swipes of eyeshadow, a few blots of lipstick, and one accidental poke in the eye with the mascara wand later, I was ready. As I passed my mother's room, I stopped in my tracks. Mom wasn't home.

I glanced at her empty room. That conversation last night was certainly about me. I didn't quite believe that Mom would send me away, but I was definitely going to ask her about what I heard. I knew my mother would never do that. Things had been weird lately, but we were friends. She wanted to be around me. She would never just send me away to let perfect strangers take care of me. Besides, this was my last year of school. And I was so close to being considered an adult. It would just be silly.

But I wondered if there was anything in her room to let me know for sure.

THE CUBBY

I WALKED INTO THE bedroom. I peeked around and did the same in the master bathroom, just to be sure the coast was clear. I strolled around the room thinking of where a good hiding place might be. The nightstand was too obvious. Underwear drawer? Mom was too modest. Under the mattress? She wasn't trying to hide her diary.

I glanced over at the closet and walked in. I looked around for a minute. She wouldn't have secrets in a shoebox—might as well have laid it all out on the bed.

I moved her hanging clothes, peering behind them. I worked my way around the length of the closet. When I got to the far end, there was a tiny metal door painted the same color as the rest of the walls. I inspected it for a minute. No handle. Hmm...

I touched it and pushed. It clicked and popped open. Well, that was easy. My heart began to race.

I opened it slowly, not knowing what I was going to find. There was a folder and a wooden box. Of course, out of curiosity, I reached for the box first. It seemed like it was handmade, with hearts carved into it. When I opened it, it began to sing some kind instrumental song. It was a music box.

The inside of the lid had a tiny mirror and the box was filled with little letters, cards, and what seemed like random trinkets. I picked out a pink ribbon and a bracelet with the word *SISTERS* engraved into it. I pulled out a folded piece of paper that almost looked like something Phoebe and I would pass around to each other under our desks in class. The front read *TO: EVIE*. I opened the letter.

Dear Evie,

Hiya. Oh my God! This class is so boring! Anyway, so did Jack sneak in last night? I fell asleep. You know if Dad found out, he would have a cow! Are we still going to the game Friday night? Or are you gonna ditch me for Jack??? You know I would love you anyway. Write me back! I'm bored!
Love Ya,
Meg

Who the hell was Meg? I knew Jack was my dad's name. But Evie? My mom's name was Veronica.

Confused, I folded the paper back up and placed it into the box. I searched a little deeper and found a Post-it that read: *Megan 760-555-7589*. I assumed this was the same 'Meg' as in the letter. And maybe even the same 'Megan' Mom mentioned on the phone last night. I stared at the Post-it before deciding to stuff it into my back pocket.

I closed the music box and pulled out the thick manila folder and opened it. The first page seemed to look like something that came from a hospital. I scanned through it quickly, suddenly realizing that I could get caught at any minute.

Grace Elizabeth Romero
Date of Birth: June 10, 2002
Diagnosis: Unknown

Romero? My last name was Shelley. Was I sick? What the hell was this?

"Gracie?"

The file fell to the floor when I heard my mother's voice from downstairs.

"Shit!" I scrambled to get all of the paperwork back into the folder.

"Gracie? Are you home, dear? I'm getting ready to make you some lunch!"

Her heels clanked up the stairs. I rushed to get the folder back into the secret cubby-hole. I closed the tiny door tightly and moved the clothes back to its original spot.

"Grace? What are you doing?"

Without turning around, I pretended to nonchalantly touch each article of clothing hanging in the closet.

"Hey, Mom. I was just looking for something to wear. I'm going to meet Phoebe at the mall today." I tried to make my voice sound as normal as possible.

"Oh, yeah? Well, here. I just bought this from that store you like on Magazine Street." She came into the closet and pulled a gray cardigan off the hanger. I couldn't look her in the eye yet. I felt that if I did, she would instantly know I was lying. I continued to glance around intently at her array of clothing. This wouldn't be farfetched. Mom was actually quite fashionable for a mom.

She handed me the cardigan and I took it without looking, which may have seemed a bit suspicious.

"Grace?" Her tone told me she knew something was up. "What's going on?"

I finally looked at her. Well, everything on her face except her eyes.

"Nothing. I just really need to get going. I told Phoebe I was going to be there soon."

I turned to leave, but she grabbed my wrist. She knew. She knew I was going through her things.

There was a pause, and then finally, she asked, "Have you eaten?"

"Yeah, I ate breakfast." In that same breath, the hunger pains began.

"Well, let me cook you something before you go. Phoebe will understand."

There was no need for any persuading. The thought of her delicious cooking was already making my mouth water.

After an exceptionally filling lunch and a whole lot of awkward silences, I headed out the door to meet Phoebe at the mall. We only lived a couple of miles away, and of course, after the delightful lunch Mom made for me, I was feeling as alive as ever. I could have walked a million miles after that amazing lunch. My body was loaded with energy.

On my way there, I thought about the past few days. One of my mother's philosophies was that when the world seemed to be too confusing, take a step back and look around. The point of this was to get a bigger picture in order to get a better understanding of the situation and to make better decisions.

Within the last seventy-two hours, Tristen and I had a date, I passed out in a very embarrassing way, Sonny threatened me, my body was mysteriously operating in some weird ways, and my mother seemed to be lying about something. So there. I took a step back and got the bigger picture.

The Tristen situation was taken care of. The plan to win him over was underway. Sonny might not have been aware of it yet, or maybe she was, but I had declared war.

My body was growing, I'd guess, from what Mom had said. But who knew? To be honest, the freaky feelings and things that were happening to me didn't seem as important as everything else. Like, for instance, my mother lying.

It sounded like she was going to send me away. I wasn't too concerned with this because I honestly didn't believe Mom would do that. Maybe she was just upset about what I did over the raw meat and found it comforting to confide in Dr. Walker.

The things I found in her closet seemed to be off, but there could be a number of reasons for those. This 'Meg' person could be a friend and 'Evie' could be a nickname? Maybe my dad was cheating on my mom when they were younger, and my mom found this letter? A little out of the box, but my point was, it could have been anything.

And about all of those medical papers. Well, that's normal for someone to have. And it was obviously when I was a kid. But what did it mean? Apparently, I was being diagnosed for something. But what was wrong? Why was it *unknown*?

The last name was a bit puzzling, but again, could have a reasonable explanation.

The question now was: should I ask my mother about her conversation last night and what I found today? I have never had to lie to my mother about anything. We always had a very open relationship. She always made me feel comfortable about telling her things. But I felt like that started changing when I told her about Tristen. And now that I knew she was lying to me about something, or rather withholding information, how would I know she wasn't holding back more? I had always been curious about my dad, whom she refused to speak of. Maybe I could find out more if I snooped again.

I suddenly remembered the Post-it I had stuck in my back pocket. I pulled it out as I entered the entrance to the mall.

Megan. I was just going to have to call Megan soon, whoever she was.

"So, what do you think?" Phoebe whispered as we both watched Eric help a customer find a shirt size.

"He's pretty hot, Phoebe." And he was. His six-feet-tall stature towered over the man he was speaking to. His muscles were screaming to get out of his uniform shirt. His black, spiky hair was perfectly sculptured. I turned my head sideways to get a better look at his jeans, which were snug to his butt. And he had a really nice butt.

Phoebe slapped me on my arm. "OKAY!"

I giggled and felt my cheeks flush. "Is that a tattoo?"

"It's tribal," Phoebe exhaled with admiration.

"No. No way, Phoebe. What happened with the last two guys who had tattoos? They were bad-boy wannabes who ended up cheating on you."

"G, he's so not like that. He's so romantic and sweet. I promise you will love him." She walked around the counter to check out a customer at the register. I turned my back to Eric.

"Phoebe, it's like you have bad luck with tattoos. You guys have only been seeing each other for, like, a day and you're already falling for him."

"Grace, don't worry. I know for sure he isn't like that."

"How do you know that? I think you should slow down with this guy. How do you know he isn't seeing someone else? How do you know he isn't juggling, like, ten girls and you, which makes eleven? How do you know he won't break your poor little already-broken-too-many-times heart?"

"Because I could never even imagine doing that to her."

I jumped at his voice. My jaw dropped and I stared at Phoebe. She gave her customer his change and smiled. I turned around slowly, trying to come up with some kind of excuse, but my brain froze.

"I'm sorry I—"

"You must be Grace," Eric said softly before leaning down to give me a kiss on my cheek. I turned my cheek toward his lips, feeling every bit of shame one could feel. He added, "I've heard a lot about you."

"Hopefully, you've heard good things. Good enough for you to forget what I just said," I said innocently.

He laughed a deep, genuine laugh. "Done. I know you're just looking out for your best friend. But I can tell you now that I'm not juggling 'like ten girls,'" he mocked. "Is that even possible?"

Phoebe came around the counter and put her arm around his waist. "I don't think so."

I blushed.

"Don't worry, Grace, I have no interest in letting this one go." He squeezed Phoebe and kissed her forehead. She smiled, and then I knew. I knew that this was different. She seemed to be in total bliss standing next to him. And that was all I wanted for her.

"Um...Grace? Look who just walked in."

I turned toward the door, and there he was. Tristen.

He walked in, stopping at the first row of shirts hanging on the rack. My heart sunk into my stomach, panic suddenly washing over me.

Phoebe interrupted my anxiety attack. "Are you gonna talk to him, silly?"

"Should I?"

"Um...yeah," Eric chimed in. "He's here by himself. And you look great. You should definitely go."

Oh, I liked this guy. I smiled nervously at Eric and Phoebe before I made my way over to where Tristen was standing.

His back was to me. I didn't want to seem like a creepy stalker and possibly scare him by coming up behind him, so I walked around to the other side of the rack while I pretended to be interested in some clothes. Now all he had to do was look up.

I peeked over at him a few times, but he seemed to be concentrating hard on what he was doing.

Come on, look at me.

I sighed. He wasn't going to look. I glanced over at Phoebe and Eric, who were motioning for me to speak first.

Okay. Just do it, Grace.

"Tristen?"

He looked up. His smile was infectious. "Grace!" he practically yelled.

I prayed my face didn't turn bright red. "Hi."

"Hi. What are you doing here?"

"Shopping." It just came out quicker than I could stop it.

"For a guy?" His smile slowly faded.

"What?" I was confused.

"Um...you're in the men's section."

I looked down at the shirt I was holding on to. Yup, it was a size XXL.

"Oh, no...I...Phoebe works...." Oh my God. What was I saying?

"Oh, yeah. That's right. Phoebe works here. Cool," Tristen confirmed.

"Yeah, I came to see her. So, what are you doing?"

"Oh, I, uh...came to shop a little." He grabbed the back of his neck. I pondered on it for a moment, and then soon remembered he did the same thing on our study date when his phone rang. Sonny was here somewhere.

I cleared my throat and glanced around the store as if to be checking things out. I would have seen her walk in with him. She couldn't be in here.

"Hey, you wanna go outside for some fresh air? I've been shopping around for, like, a million hours."

"Wow! Aren't guys allergic to shopping?"

"Well, not this guy. I deserve new clothes sometimes, too. So, you wanna go?"

I glanced over at Phoebe and Eric, who had now completely forgotten about me and had focused all their attention on each other. I watched as they gave each other flirty looks. I wanted that. I could have that.

"Yes. Let's go."

THE BENCH

WE WALKED OUT OF the clothing store and made our way to the exit. Nothing was said, but Tristen seemed to be looking around nervously, probably hoping that Sonny wouldn't pop out of somewhere.

We finally got outside and found a bench nestled in a corner, away from the exit door. *How perfect,* I thought. Away from psycho girlfriends finding us.

We sat down and Tristen pushed his bags to the side.

"Man, I don't know how you girls can shop for a whole day. It's really exhausting!"

"We were built for this kind of stuff. It's in our DNA, you know."

He chuckled. "Well, how about you do all the shopping for me?"

"Me? I don't know what you like. Or your size, or anything."

That was a complete lie. I have been paying attention to his threads for quite some time.

"Oh, you'll learn that I'm pretty easy. Jeans and a T-shirt. Sometimes a hat or maybe even a cute little cardigan like that," he teased, poking mc in my ribs.

I squirmed and giggled. Wow. Could I have been any more of a girl?

I felt like I had to explain my choice in clothing today. I didn't know I was going to run into him.

"Oh...I wasn't even planning on coming to the mall. It was a last-minute thing," I lied as I looked away.

"What are you talking about?" He lifted a leg on the wooden bench and turned toward me. "I think you look adorable." He pointed at my shoes. "And you wear *Chucks*! That's pretty hot."

It felt as though my heart was going to pump the blood completely out of my cheeks. Did he just call me hot?

Okay, now isn't the time to be shy, Grace. He is obviously letting you know he digs you.

I looked down at my hands.

Grace, fidgeting is not any better.

Suddenly, his finger swept my long curl from the front of my face and placed it behind my ear.

"Your hair is a whole other thing," he said softly with a smile.

I couldn't turn away. Our eyes locked, and for once, my heart froze. Every other thought flew out of my mind. It was as if everything else melted around us. There wasn't anything I wanted more than for his lips to touch mine.

What was it about this guy? He was a normal high school senior. Sure, he was a jock and popular and sweet and super sexy and polite and cool, but there were a ton of guys like that out there. Why was I completely obsessed with everything Tristen?

A car horn sounded in the distance and Tristen broke the staring contest. Damn it!

He cleared his throat before he spoke. "So, this weekend coming up is finally Halloween. Are you excited for all of us to hang out?"

He had no idea. "Oh, yeah. Like I said, Halloween is my favorite."

"What are you going to be?"

"I was thinking about a vampire. Or maybe a zombie."

"Definitely a zombie. People love zombies," he stated.

"What about you?" I asked, really curious to know if he had a creative imagination.

"Well, how about a zombie?"

I laughed. Really?

"No, seriously. If you're a zombie, then I'm a zombie. It would happen anyway if it were real, right?"

"What? That if I'm a zombie, then you're a zombie?" I asked, genuinely confused.

"Yeah. I mean, if you were a zombie, then I would eventually become one. Especially if we were sitting this close to each other. You would bite me, wouldn't you?"

I wasn't sure if I was imagining it or if he was slowly moving in closer to me. Was his comment supposed to mean more than I thought it meant? I was bewildered and eager at the same time. But before I knew it, my mouth unconsciously ruined the moment.

"Well, it depends on how you could catch the zombie virus. I could spread it to you the good old fashion way by biting you. Although, there are other ways. You may already have the virus. Or, it may be an airborne virus. Either way, if zombies were real, you wouldn't be doomed. People could still survive. They would just have to be extra careful. Stock up on pipe bombs, guns, sniper rifles are a must, Molotov cocktails...you get the picture. Food, medical supplies, and all that stuff, of course. Chances are, people won't know right away how the virus came about, so making sure to stay clean, be aware of any wounds on your body, and keeping your mouth closed in the process of killing zombies would help. You know, protection from splatter."

Tristen's facial expression was a mixture of confusion, delight, surprise, and what seemed to be total awe.

Crap. I went too far. He thought I was some kind of freak. I looked down at my fingers in embarrassment.

"So, you have been thinking about this a lot, huh? You weren't kidding when you said you loved horror movies."

"I kind of have a weird thing for stuff like that. Let's just say that you can never be too sure," I nearly whispered and shrugged my shoulders.

He chuckled and lifted my chin with his finger. "You are so adorable."

His smile was intoxicating.

Before I could respond with a witty and even more adorable remark, a horrific screech rang through my ears.

"TRISTEN!"

We both turned around instantly, although I knew neither of us wanted to. Sonny was standing a few feet away with her shopping bags in hand. Her facial expression was proof that the devil lived somewhere deep within all of her perfect clothes and makeup.

"Sonny, I was just—"

"You were just what, Tristen? Checking her pulse?"

What? Certainly, she knew that one could not check for a pulse on the chin. At least I hoped she knew that.

Tristen obviously caught it, too. He chuckled. "What? No, Sonny. Come on, let's just finish shopping," he said, clearly annoyed that she had caught us. He stood up from the bench and turned to me. "I'll call you," he murmured.

"Well, what if I don't want to go right now?" she said through her teeth.

"Sonny, let's go. You know I have a meet tonight. I don't have time for this."

Wow. He seemed to be kind of pissed. Sonny didn't say anything. Instead, she gave me the evil eye and turned to follow Tristen back into the mall.

I sat on the bench a while longer, trying to relive the past fifteen minutes in my mind. I didn't even know where to start. He liked me. I knew for sure now that he liked me. But what the hell was that with Sonny? He just told her what to do and without hesitation, she did it. For a split second, she almost resembled a puppy being scolded for peeing on the carpet. For some strange reason, my sympathy nerve struck. I would have to investigate this a little. I certainly didn't want to feel bad for Sonny, but I needed to understand why Tristen always seemed so irritated with her.

Or maybe he just had to be that way when dealing with Sonny.

After people-watching outside for some time, I walked back into the mall and headed toward Phoebe's store. As I passed the food court, Phoebe's voice yelled over the crowd. She must have been on her lunch break.

I searched through the sea of people until I spotted her waving a hand in the air. She and Eric were at a table right in the middle of the food court. It was a Saturday afternoon, busy day for the mall, and people were everywhere—either waiting in line or waiting for a table to become available. I maneuvered my way around, trying to avoid the smell of food when I felt my stomach begin to growl. I was going to leave after I visited with Phoebe a bit, so hopefully there wouldn't be any more fainting and making a total ass of myself.

Phoebe and I finally locked eyes right when I made it a few feet away from her table.

Next thing I knew, I felt my body lift up off the ground and I could suddenly see my legs in front of my face. On my way down, I watched my shoe fly off my foot. Before I could see where it landed, my head and back smacked into the marble floor. The sound was deafening on my end, but apparently to everyone else as well. The entire food court stopped eating, ordering, even talking, and turned in my direction. I could make out a few laughs and someone even blurting out, "Oh, shit!"

I stayed sprawled out on the floor for what seemed like an eternity before I realized that I had fallen. My head instantly began to throb. I winced and reached behind my head to somehow ease the pain with my hand.

"Grace!"

Phoebe's voice sounded far, far away, even though she was only a few feet from me. She ran over with Eric by her side. They immediately helped me up from the ground.

"Grace, are you okay?"

"Ugh...yeah...I think so."

"What a shame."

Phoebe, Eric, and I turned around to see who would say such a thing.

Sonny was sitting at a nearby table, her chin resting on her hands. She laughed. "Let me tell you what happened! I ordered a slice of pizza from that pizza place, right?" She pointed at *Tony's Pizzeria*. "And as I was walking over to my table, I dropped the darn thing. I guess you slipped on it, Grace. What a shame. Tony's pizza is really good."

"You asshole!" Phoebe lunged herself at Sonny, but before she could even move an inch, Eric grabbed her by the waist.

"Well, I guess I'm gonna head out. Tristen's waiting for me, if you know what I mean," Sonny said, dangling a pink bag from *Victoria's Secret* on her finger. She stood up from the table and waltzed out of the food court as if nothing even happened.

"Damn it, Eric! Let me go! I can catch that skinny bitch!"

"Phoebe, she's gone. It won't help. This is what she wants you to do." Eric's voice was calming.

Phoebe eventually stopped squirming and tended back to her best friend's sorry state of being damaged, embarrassed, and void of any dignity. At least I became boring enough for everyone around to go on about their business.

"No, Grace. I can tell you want to give up. I can see it in your face," Phoebe asserted as she held onto my elbow, supporting me. My head was killing me, but my back felt worse. I struggled to keep a balance. Eric was back at her side a minute later with my shoe in hand.

"You might need this," he said.

I managed a chuckle and reached for my shoe. Phoebe, on the other hand, was without humor.

I sat down on a chair and watched as Phoebe bent down to put my shoe back on. Tristen's favorite shoe.

"Phoebe. Enough," I finally said. "She is a bitch. But what am I going to do? Ask her to meet me in the schoolyard so we can fight?"

"Yes! She deserves an ass kicking. If you don't, I will."

"Phoebe, don't worry, I'm working on it."

I began to feel exasperated with Phoebe. I knew that her heart was in the right place. It was actually very flattering that she wanted to protect me. After all, I would do the same for her. But I knew what I had to do. Tristen was obviously into me. There was no doubt that before our romantic moment was sorely interrupted by the evil girlfriend, he was definitely wearing his heart on his sleeve for me. The ultimate revenge would be the day Tristen breaks up with her to be with me. It was just a matter of when that would happen.

After Phoebe continued on with her rant about kicking some Sonny ass, I walked back to their store and said my goodbyes. Phoebe warned me that if Sonny pulled another bitch stunt, she was going to "let all hell break loose on her face," with or without my consent. Eric, on the other hand, seemed to understand where I was coming from. He agreed that karma would eventually catch up with Sonny, and he defended me when I tried to explain to Phoebe that resorting to violence was not the answer. I didn't want to physically hurt Sonny.

Truthfully, mental pictures of my hands around her throat and hearing her plead to be free did flood my mind. But I was not a violent person. All I wanted was one thing. And I was starting to get the aching feeling that he wanted me, too.

THE CAT

IT WAS A GORGEOUS Fall dusk. On my walk home, I thought about how Tristen tucked my hair behind my ears. Flashbacks of his touch on my chin burned into my memory. I grabbed it and smiled. Hopefully soon there would be more of those memories engraved into my mind.

I was about three blocks away from home when I felt the same, gnawing pain in the pit of my stomach. I cringed and automatically hugged myself.

God. I was so tired of this feeling. How was I hungry again? I had only been gone for about two hours.

The gnawing in my stomach grew more intense with every step I took. I began to pick up the pace, knowing that Mom had some dinner cooking on the stove at that very moment. I swore I could actually smell it. My head began to ache, along with all the muscles in my body. Sweat started to fall from the roots of my hair, and my pores were beginning to smell.

What the hell was happening to me? Normally, I would have a little while before I felt this bad from hunger, but it seemed to be coming on more quickly—and stronger.

I found myself practically running. But my body didn't seem to like that too much and slowed its pace on its own. I started to breathe heavily, and everything from my toenails to my teeth began throbbing.

My vision began blurring, but from the corner of my eye, I spotted a shadow in someone's driveway. I came to a halt and turned my head. The darkness was coming on fast, but the streetlights and the house that belonged to the driveway were not lit up just yet. From what I could tell, the shadow was small and motionless. I slowly crept toward it, hunching over just a bit to get a better view of what the shadow could be—not that my body could even help it.

As I approached, there was finally movement and I caught a glimpse of yellow eyes staring back at me.

Meow.

The moment I was sure that something was there, my mind took complete control. The hunger was debilitating and thoughts of what I had to do to get some food in my stomach crowded my brain.

As I got closer, the cat changed from the prone position to sitting, purring and meowing some more. It didn't seem scared of me.

"Hi, little guy," I said quietly. Those were the last words I would be able to speak until I got what I needed.

This cat was extremely brave because he came over to me and wrapped himself around my ankles. He rubbed his body on my legs and meowed a few more times.

I bent down to give him a rub the best my bones would let me. I smiled at his innocence. Animals don't have a care in the world. Their only concern is living.

Another terrible pain shot through me. I clenched my jaw and fought a scream that was ready to fly out of my throat. I rubbed the kitty's little head with more urgency. I wasn't sure what possessed me to stop here and love on this little guy instead of making my way to some food. Every movement my hand made to rub the cat only brought on my hunger even more.

I continued rubbing his tiny neck with more and more exigency. Something started to smell appealing and surprisingly familiar to me. I lifted my nose in the air like a hound to get a better whiff. I closed my eyes and tried to mentally figure out the similarity. It was coppery...bitter. My mouth watered as I thought about what it could be. When I brought my head back down to look at the cat, the smell got stronger. I bowed down closer and realized what it was. The meat. This cat smelled exactly like the raw meat I ate this morning.

Unconsciously, I tightened my grip around the cat's neck.

What am I doing? I need to get home.

The cat tried to claw its way out of my hand, but I couldn't let go.

Oh my God. Grace! Let go. Let go!

He pulled back as my grip got tighter and tighter.

Grace, what are you doing? Leave him alone!

And before I knew it, there was a crackling sound and the cat's body no longer resisted. Before my mind could register what I'd done, I picked up the limp, lost soul and hobbled over to the sidewalk in search of a dark corner. About one and a half blocks from where I resided, I found a dark house with a for-sale sign on the lawn. The porch was deep and dim. I was sure no one could find me there.

I staggered up the four steps to the porch and huddled into a corner, resting the cat on my lap.

Okay. I had just ended this poor cat's life. Parts of me were feeling sorrow for the little guy and anger at myself, but my stomach felt otherwise. I needed to do this. My bones ached for this. I couldn't live without this. I wanted this.

With that last thought, I brought the cat's body to my mouth and bit down. Its body rested in my hands like a ragdoll, and with the first bite, blood oozed out through my fingers and onto my legs.

The taste was even better than I'd imagined. Even though the smell of it was almost the same as the raw meat I ate at home, the taste was completely different. It was warm and juicy and so soft. With every bite, I sunk my face deeper and deeper into its little body. My eyes rolled in the back of my head as I swallowed the bitterly delicious red liquid. The meat was easy to chew, and every swallow brought me into some kind of euphoria. It was almost as if I could feel my brain cells awakening. My senses were growing stronger with every grind of my jaw. My mind briefly confirmed that this was by far the best thing I had ever gotten my hands on.

I sat in the dark, draining every ounce of blood and flesh the cat had to offer. Not one thought of my life entered my mind. In that moment, no one existed except me and this carcass. There were no glimpses of Mom, Phoebe, school, Sonny, my dad, or even Tristen. All I needed—all I wanted—was right here.

When I finally regained control, my eyes focused on what was in my lap. Bones and pieces of fleshy tissue were scattered all around me. The collar that I must have thrown to the side during my feast was a foot away from me. I reached over to pick it up. A tag dangled, engraved with the name *Fluffy*.

I quickly threw it away as if it had caught fire.

Grace, what did you do?

I swiped the aftermath off my body and shot up to my feet.

Grace, what did you do!

Tears began to leak out of my eyes when I realized what horrible thing I had done. I just killed a cat! And I ate it! What had I done?

I ran off the porch of the vacant home and into the direction of my house. I could see my mom's car in the driveway and a wave of relief swept over me. She was home. She would know what to do. She would know how to explain why I just killed and ate a freaking cat.

I swung open the door, winded and crying at the same time. I shut the door and stood in the foyer, unable to understand what just happened.

"Gracie, is that you? Dinner is ready, honey!" she yelled from the kitchen.

I didn't move an inch. I wasn't hungry.

"Grace?"

What did I just do?

Mom walked out of the kitchen with a couple of plates in her hands. She halted to a dead stop when she saw me.

"Grace!"

The plates dropped to the floor, shattering into pieces and echoing throughout the house.

"What happened? Why are you covered in blood?"

I glanced down at myself. I didn't realize how much blood I had on me. How could something so small have so much blood?

Mom slowly walked over to me, as if she were approaching a bomb. She held out her hands.

"Grace, honey. Talk to me. What...happened?"

I didn't know how to respond. What should I say? I was walking along the road and found a cute cat. I killed it and ate. Normally, a kid would come home and say, "Mom, I found a cat. Can we keep him?" No, I ate the damn thing.

My eyes were wide, and my heart was still pounding. The crying subsided and I believe what I was feeling was shock.

"Grace, are you hurt?"

I looked over at her and shook my head. She proceeded to get closer, finally resting her hands on my shoulders.

"Okay, let's go upstairs and get you into the bathtub." Her voice became calmer.

I finally felt soothed, nodding my head without a word. She guided me upstairs into my bathroom where she ran a warm bath and helped me out of my blood-stained clothes.

I soaked in the tub while Mom rinsed my jeans out in the sink. I finally broke the deafening silence.

"I don't understand," I said softly, looking down in shame.

She stopped her rinsing and looked over at me. "What don't you understand, Gracie?" she asked with genuine concern. She seemed to be so calm. I was sure she'd be hysterical when she saw blood all over me.

She knelt down against the tub and waited for me to answer. I took a deep breath and swallowed hard. How was I going to tell her I literally ate a cat?

"Mom, I did something horrible." The tears started stinging the corners of my eyes.

"Honey, I'm sure whatever you did there was a reason for it." She took the loofah and began scrubbing my back. I shrugged away.

"Mom, you don't understand. *I* don't understand." My voice went hoarse.

"Gracie, just tell me and we'll fix it. We always do." She was right.

My tears came down in full force as I braced myself for what I was about to reveal. The thing was that I wasn't sure why I was even going to tell her the truth. I could have just lied and said that, I don't know, I started my period or something.

But the truth was that I felt lost. I had no idea why I did what I did, but Mom would always come to the rescue. She would always understand, never judge—unless it was about Tristen—and she always knew how to make me feel better about the situation. She did always fix everything.

"When I was walking home from the mall, I got really, really hungry," I said without looking at her. I couldn't look at her. As much as she never judged me about other things, I knew she would when I dropped the bomb on this one.

She was quiet.

"I saw a cat. A black cat with yellow eyes." My tears were now waterfalls.

"...and...I...I petted it, but my stomach was so hungry...so I squeezed his neck until he was...and I just had to, Mom. I had to." I finally looked at her. Her face was composed. There was no expression. This made me cry harder. What the hell was she thinking? If she had any thoughts of sending me away, this would surely bring her to a decision.

"Shh...it's okay, Gracie," she said serenely as she continued to scrub and rinse my body. There was no change in her motions. My tears were coming on so strong that I felt they could probably fill up the rest of the tub. But she was as cool as a cucumber. And it pissed me off.

"Mom, I just killed a cat! AND ATE IT!" I yelled so loud that it hurt my throat. "How can you be so relaxed right now?" I pushed her away and stood up, covering my private areas with my hands.

"Grace, it's okay. Just please calm down and we can talk about this—"

"No! It's not okay! Something is wrong with me, Mother! Something horrible! How can I do this? I couldn't control myself! I couldn't even think about what I was doing! Weren't you a doctor? Can't you help me?" I asked, desperation the only emotion I could express.

My throat was killing me. I have never yelled at my mother this way. I would never even think about yelling at her. But what the hell was she thinking? How could she not be freaking out as much as I was?

I stepped out of the tub and rushed to my room. I needed to get out of there. I threw on a pair of jeans, a sweatshirt, and my *Chucks*—the ones that weren't drenched in blood. I threw my hair into a messy bun and grabbed my phone.

"Gracie, where do you think you're going?" Mom asked, this time with a hint of authority.

"Out." I walked out of my room and headed towards the stairs. Mom followed.

"Grace, listen to me. We have to talk about this. You need to eat something!"

I stopped. Was she serious? I turned around and gave her the craziest eyes I could manage so that she would get just how crazy I thought she sounded. "Are you kidding me? How in the hell can you honestly be worried about food right now?"

"Grace Elizabeth, do not take that tone with me!" she yelled back.

"How can I not? Are you that selfish? What? Did you cook something different tonight and you need me to try it? You need my validation? Guess what, Mother! All of your obsessions with cooking isn't going to change the fact that Dad left you!"

She literally took two steps back. I could almost see the dagger I just stabbed through her heart. She seemed like she had a million things to say, but nothing left her mouth. I instantly wanted to take it back. I didn't even know why I said it. Maybe it was just a button I felt I could push.

We stood for a moment, silently, and stared each other straight in the eyes. Finally, I turned on my heels and rushed down the stairs. I didn't look back, but I was pretty sure she didn't move an inch either.

I flew down the porch steps and hooked a left down the sidewalk. I had no idea where I was going, but I needed to just get away.

THE BASKETBALL

WHAT THE HELL WAS happening to me? I ate a freaking cat less than an hour ago. AN ACTUAL CAT! My emotions were everywhere. I was upset, sad, and so confused. But my body hadn't felt this great in a couple of weeks. A brief thought of wanting to run a marathon popped into my head, but I quickly crushed it because that was ridiculous to think about.

My body felt...rejuvenated. Exhilarated. I could hear a car alarm in the distance. I could see a person walking down the street a few blocks down perfectly. And I could swear, as I power-walked, there was a skip in each step. It felt like a hip-hop song was pumping through my veins. If someone saw me right now, they would definitely think I was cracked out for sure.

Okay, Grace...chill.

I tried to slow my pace to give myself time to think.

What was going on? Let's think this through. Let's replay everything that had been happening over the past couple of weeks. There had to be a pattern somewhere. It couldn't be hormones. I had never seen, heard, or read of any girl who just started eating random cats around the neighborhood because of her period.

Let's go backwards and work our way to where it started.

Tonight, I ate a cat.

Okay...that was about the only thing I could really think about. I ate a cat!

The night brought a strong breeze through the air. I unconsciously zipped up my sweatshirt, but I wasn't cold.

I was walking so fast that I didn't realize I'd been walking toward school. I was about two blocks away when I could hear a basketball bouncing and tennis shoes scrapping against the concrete.

I really didn't want to see anyone from school. But if I stayed on this path, it would eventually lead to the lake, which was really where I wanted to be.

At Middleton High, there were some guys playing basketball on the outside court near the gym. I could just walk past and keep my eyes lowered. Hopefully, I wouldn't get noticed. I threw my hood over my head and sped up my power walk.

Suddenly, the ball flew over the fence, bouncing right at my feet. All the guys stopped and glanced in my direction.

"Aw, Kasey! You're going to get it this time."

"Oh, wait! Someone's right there. Excuse me! Could you throw us our ball back?"

I stopped and stood in front of it, contemplating on whether or not I should be a jerk and just walk away. Whatever. I knew who they were, but they couldn't tell who I was. I could just ignore them.

I started to take another step when I heard a familiar voice.

"Kasey, just go get it. That ball could've hit that person in the head because you don't know how to play," Tristen said.

I looked down at the ball again with a sudden desire to see Tristen's beautiful face. I picked it up and took a deep breath. I turned toward the court, purposely positioning myself in the light. It didn't take Tristen long to recognize me.

A grin emerged from his lips when he realized it was me. "Grace?"

I smiled as I watched him walk over to the fence. His hair was messy, and he looked all athletic with his sleeveless jersey and gray sweatpants. His arms were bare, and I could see a small tattoo on his deltoid.

I had no idea he had a tattoo. And I had just lectured Phoebe on guys with tattoos. But something told me Tristen wouldn't break my heart.

I couldn't quite make out what the tattoo was, but I didn't want to stare at it, either. I didn't want to be one of those girls who were like, "OMG, can I touch it?"

It was hot, though.

"Hey! What are you doing here?" he asked.

"Oh, I needed a walk. What about you?"

Seriously, Grace? He's playing basketball, you idiot.

"Just hanging out with the guys."

Obviously.

"Wow, so you really *are* a jock," I said playfully.

He chuckled. "Yeah, well...what can I say? I love wearing sweaty jockstraps. So, listen, about today and the whole Sonny thing..."

I wasn't sure if he was talking about getting caught with me outside on the bench or Sonny purposely trying to destroy me in the food court. I chose to believe he was talking about being caught because I knew for a fact she wouldn't confess to what she did to me.

"Hey, don't mention it." I shrugged. "I would be a little pissed too if I saw my boyfriend talking to a girl with great hair."

His smile grew wider. "Modestly conceited. I like that."

"It's the only way to be."

He put one hand on the chain-link fence, poking his fingers through. "Seriously, you do have great hair."

"I know."

Nice one, Grace!

His eyes lit up.

"Hey, Miles! Are we playing or what? We kind of need the ball back!"

Tristen turned around, and then back to me. I threw the ball over the fence and he caught it without even looking. Impressive.

"So...I'm just about done with this game. You want some company?"

The butterflies in my stomach were doing pirouettes.

"Sure."

I got the aching feeling that his butterflies were doing the same. I couldn't imagine his smile getting any wider than it was.

"Awesome. Just give me a sec. I kind of smell, so I'm gonna rush in and take a quick shower."

"I didn't even know school was open this late," I said. Seriously, no clue.

"Well, we're the jocks, remember? We kind of get to do whatever we want."

"Oh, well...excuse me," I said, holding my hands up. "Now who is being conceited?"

He winked at me and turned toward the gym. He was so unbelievably sexy.

I backed away from the fence and stuck my hands in my sweatshirt pockets. For a moment, I completely forgot about the feline feast and started to concentrate on the right things to say while we shared our walk. I had the tendency to sound like I smoked too many weed cigarettes when I was around Tristen. I stated the obvious about things, and I certainly didn't want him to think I was boring.

I watched the basketball game and compared those guys to Tristen. Why was I so attracted to him? I obviously didn't know him that well. I mean, his looks would definitely be a great reason to like him so much. But I wasn't shallow. I needed more than that.

And after watching Tristen over the past few years, I could kind of get who he was. I had seen him open doors for teachers, study hard, bring Sonny a balloon and a teddy bear on her birthday, help out his teammates, and tutor some of the students from the middle school tutoring program. This clearly proved that chivalry was not dead in his book. He was determined. He was thoughtful. He was kind. And he had a warm heart.

But I wanted to know him better. I wanted to know about his life, his family, and his thoughts. And let's face it, getting to know him intimately wasn't such a bad idea, either.

It literally felt like he took five seconds to shower and get dressed before he came back out of the gym. He was now wearing some jeans, a hoodie, and...well, what do you know? *Chucks.* This made me smile. His hair was still messy, which made me even happier. He had great hair, too.

"Where are you going, hoss?"

"Just taking a walk. Hey, rematch tomorrow night?"

"Yeah, if Sonny lets you," Kasey said.

"Dude, you know she ain't letting him go nowhere," Dexter chimed in.

"I'll be here at eight," Tristen said as he continued to stroll over to the fence.

"We'll see." Kasey didn't seem at all convinced.

What? He wasn't allowed to hang out with his friends? I didn't get it.

He met me on the other side of the fence, and we stood face to face, hands in our pockets. He then pulled his hood over his head. I smiled, and so did he.

"So, where are we walking to?"

"I was thinking about going to the lake. Is that okay?" I asked.

"Yeah, that's cool with me."

We began our walk. There was silence for the first two minutes, and I wasn't sure how to start the conversation.

"So, how was your day?" he asked.

Good. He broke the ice.

I instantly thought of poor kitty and the sound of its neck bones shattering in my hands. "Um…it was okay."

He sensed my hesitation. "Wanna talk about it?"

"Not really," I said, hoping that he would just drop it. I knew I would have to lie to him, but for some reason I found it may be extremely hard to do so. Hopefully, he would sense that I really didn't want to talk about it and let it go.

"Well, if you do, you can tell me. I'm all ears."

"Thanks." I briefly considered his invitation but decided that it would be insane. So I changed the subject before I mouthed off anything. "Do you guys play at night often?"

"Yeah. It's not practice or anything. I'm actually not that big into basketball, but it's a good workout and a chance to hang out with the boys."

"And be jocks?"

"Exactly. You know, we trade jockstraps sometimes," he said without breaking a beat. For a second, I thought he was serious. I looked over at him in horror, but once I noticed he was visibly trying hard to keep a straight face, I couldn't hold in my laughter.

The walk over to our destination was short. The levee, otherwise known as a man-made water barrier, blocked our view of the water.

But just a few long strides over and short steps coming down the other side revealed the seemingly endless lake. We walked to the steps of the lake's edge and took our seats. There was only one streetlamp behind us, and it wasn't lit. The moon was the only light reflecting off the lake water. It was calm, softly slapping the last visible step. I inhaled the brackish smell.

I took a quick glance around to see if there were any other people trying to escape their own lives. There was usually a late-night fisherman or two trying to catch some catfish. But tonight, there seemed to be no one in our view.

Perfect. Just Tristen and me.

THE LAKE

"WOW, IT'S BEAUTIFUL OUT," he said while looking up at the sky. I glanced up with him and noticed the millions of stars scattered in the night sky. The moon was bright and hung over our heads. It *was* beautiful out. "Do you come out here often?"

"Is that a line?" I asked, allowing my wit to take over. He smiled, showing his perfect, white teeth.

"I can do better than that."

My heart fluttered. "I come out here sometimes. I like the sound of the water. It doesn't crash like waves at a beach. It's soft. It's soothing," I said, peering out into it.

"What do you think about when you're here?"

"Um...nothing really," I said, trying to remember what I actually did think about. Tonight, I would have been trying to figure out the method to my madness, but other nights I would just sit and stare out into the water, not thinking much.

"Well, that can't be true. You have to think about something," he said. He turned to face me. "Grace, tell me your innermost thoughts."

I wasn't sure if he was trying to be funny or serious this time. It was dark, but I could see his face from the light of the moon. I just couldn't read it.

"Why would you want to know that?"

"Because...I want to know you." He smiled gently at me. I got goosebumps down my back.

"Only if you tell me yours." I decided to play along.

"Touché. Let's see..." He looked away for a moment as if concentrating really hard. "Okay. I sometimes wonder why I am here."

I brought my eyebrows together in confusion. "What do you mean?"

He turned back to me to explain. "Well, sometimes I wonder why I am the way I am, and why I'm here...living. Why was I created? What am I supposed to do with my life?"

"Wow, that's deep." It was the only thing I could say. But his thoughts did begin to creep into mine. Maybe he was on to something. "So, you mean, what's your destiny?"

"Something like that. I think everyone is here for some reason. Whether it's for something big or small. Sometimes, people are here to make a difference in the whole world, while other times a person is here to make a difference in one person's life." He looked out into the lake. "Doesn't it seem like every person you have ever known has had someone make an impact in their lives? It could have been their grandma, their best friend, their teacher. It seems like we're destined to change another person's life in one way or another. Sometimes it's for the worse, but most times it's for the good."

"So, who has impacted your life?" I wouldn't think it'd be Sonny, but I was desperately hoping he wouldn't say her.

"My grandfather."

There was a noticeable pain in his eyes when he said this. My heart hurt for him and I thought about why that could be. Was he close to him? Did he pass away?

I chose not to ask anything about it.

"What about you?" he asked.

It was my turn to stare deeply into the water. As I thought about it, I couldn't come up with anyone in particular. My dad left when I was too young. I was really pissed with my mom at the moment, but from remembering my life with her, I couldn't quite place an occasion when I felt like she impacted me really. She was my mother. She was supposed to give me advice and be there for me. Phoebe was my best friend, but I didn't feel she was mature enough to impact me.

The question began to make me feel sad when I realized there really wasn't anyone in my life who had impacted me. Good or bad.

"I guess no one."

Tristen put a hand on my knee and my breath caught. "It's okay. It just hasn't happened yet."

"Well, how do you know?" I asked, now concerned that maybe I didn't catch it when it happened.

He kept his hand on my knee. "You just know. You just know that you'll never forget that person. That person will always be in your thoughts, no matter what happens. You'll remember a distinct conversation or something that transpired between the two of you that'll squeeze your heart when you think about it. You'll just...know."

"Are you wondering who you're going to impact?"

"Exactly." He smiled and squeezed my knee. His touch sent chills through my body. And when he removed his hand and placed it back into his pocket, I wanted to yell at him not to.

I thought about everything he had just said. It was a concept that I had really never thought about. But it made absolute sense to me.

Who will leave a lasting memory in my mind? Who will impact me so much that it could change decisions I make? Who would mold me? Who would influence me? And vice versa?

It seemed I needed some kind of good impact right now in my life.

"You're thinking about it now, aren't you?" he asked.

I smiled and twisted toward him. "Actually, yes. I think you might have impacted me just now."

He smiled widely. "Maybe."

"I have a question for you, Tristen." I decided to be brave. What did I have to lose anyway? I ate a cat tonight. And if I wanted to keep this war going strong with Sonny, I had to start stepping up my game.

He turned his whole body toward me, completely intrigued. "Shoot."

"What's up with what your friends were saying tonight? About Sonny not letting you go play?" Okay, I downplayed it a bit. My intension was to ask him why he was even dating Sonny. If I asked him that, there was a risk of insulting him or pissing him off.

His smile dropped and he instantly looked irritated.

Crap. I pissed him off.

"Sorry. I didn't mean to upset you," I apologized.

"No, you didn't make me upset. It's just..." He sighed. "I don't know what to do with her."

Oh, this was good. I didn't say a word.

"I mean, I care about her. We've been dating for so long, you know?"

I nodded.

"When I first moved here from Oregon, my parents were too busy working and I didn't know anyone. She kind of took me under her wing. It was great for the first year. Her friends were welcoming. She showed me around. But then she just became this demanding, self-centered, its-all-about-me chick. At that point, I just didn't know how to let go. I guess I was just...comfortable. You know what I mean?"

He scanned my eyes for an answer. Honestly, I didn't have one. I had never been in his situation. But it made me think of his aggressiveness that afternoon.

"Is that why you were mean to her today?" I asked.

"You thought I was mean to her?" he asked, surprised.

"Well, I guess a little. I mean, don't get me wrong, I know she can be—"

"A bitch," he finished.

I nodded. He said it, not me.

He took a deep breath as if he knew exactly what I was talking about. "Sometimes, she just upsets me. I would never treat a girl badly or with malice in my heart, but man, she can push my buttons sometimes."

I nodded again. He was venting and needed someone to understand, even if they really didn't.

He gazed out into the water again before saying anything. I studied his profile in the moonlight. This guy was truly a perfect specimen. His strong jawline aligned perfectly with his chin. His tan skin looked so smooth, I had to fight the urge to caress his cheek. His messy hair moved slowly with the breeze around his hoodie. I watched his subtle Adam's apple move up and down with every swallow.

He turned to look at me and I quickly turned toward the lake.

"So, what about you?" he asked.

"What about me?"

"Are you...seeing anyone?"

A *really?* chuckle escaped my throat. "No!"

"No? That's surprising!"

I whipped my head around. "Surprising? Why? Should I be?"

His face softened as he brought a hand up to my face. He swiped away a few loose pieces of hair that managed their way out of my messy bun. My pulse quickened. He really needed to stop doing that.

Or not.

"This hair... Let me see it."

"What?"

"Come on! Take your hair down. Beautiful hair like that shouldn't be tamed."

He was serious.

I stared at him a moment and thought about how much I hated being put on the spot. Did he like my hair that much?

But I did what I was told and pulled my hoodie back. With a quick slip of my hair tie, my curls came crashing down. His face lit up and his smile became devilish. I, on the other hand, wish I had a shell to crawl into. My shyness rushed through me.

He gently grabbed a handful of my hair and squeezed. It was still damp from the attempt at a bath earlier. Thankfully, Mom was able to wash the blood off my body, and none of it got in my hair.

"Your hair is amazing. Have I told you that before?"

"As a matter of fact, you have."

His hand found my cheek and he did exactly what I wanted him to do. My goosebumps came back with full force and I unconsciously leaned into him. It felt so right to lean into him. My forehead rested on his cheek as his hand cradled the side of my face. All I had to do was look up and my lips would be inches from his.

A hint of his clean cologne made its way up my nostrils.

I could do this. I could do—

I quickly twisted my body away so that I wouldn't get any vomit on him.

"Grace, are you okay?"

I felt his hand on my back.

Oh my God! What the hell did I just do!

I couldn't stop, couldn't catch my breath. I briefly thanked the night for the darkness so that he couldn't see my spew. I was sure it would be crimson red and full of cat chunks.

He continued to rub my back until I was done. It was so embarrassing, but I couldn't help it.

I wiped my mouth with the back of my sleeve before I turned back toward him.

"Come on. Let's get you home," he said with worry as we stood up and he wrapped his arm around my waist.

I didn't say anything.

We walked home in silence. He insisted that he drive me to my house since his car was repaired and parked at school, but I refused. The cool breeze on my face was refreshing. Plus, spending as much time with him as I could was my ultimate goal.

We reached my house and stopped just before my porch.

"I'm really sorry you were sick tonight."

"It's okay. I think I just ate something bad today. Thanks for keeping me company. It really helped me take my mind off things." And that was the honest truth.

"Anytime." He smiled.

I smiled too. My stomach flipped. Oh, God. It wasn't butterflies.

"Well, I really need to get going. Thanks again, Tristen for—"

He grabbed my hand. "No, Grace. I mean it. Anytime. Okay?"

He pulled me closer to him. His eyes never left mine.

This was it. Vomit breath and all. I was going to kiss Tristen Miles. We moved closer to one another, almost in slow motion. The world stopped around us once again, and my lips puckered. He was calm and sexy and oozing smolder while I felt like I was about to explode.

My heart throbbed like a jackhammer and all I could think was how amazing this was going to be.

"Gracie!"

I shut my eyes and exhaled violently. My mother.

"Grace, I've been worried sick! It's getting cold, please come in."

Tristen's eyes remained on mine.

"Grace?"

He began to back away slowly, holding on to my hand as long as he could reach it. When he finally let go, he smiled his famous smile and headed back to school.

My feet stayed grounded for another minute before I could move them. When I finally did, I saw Mom standing in the doorway with her arms crossed. I rolled my eyes. Her timing was perfection.

I headed up to the front door, eyes focused on everything but her. She knew I was pissed. I *was* pissed. There was a little twinge of guilt for what I said to her before I stormed out of the house, but I was still pissed.

Before I could step onto the first step of our staircase, I couldn't help but peek over into the kitchen. Of course, the dining room table was covered in dishes filled with food. Okay, I was mad, but not mad enough to skip a meal.

I headed into the kitchen, ready to devour every morsel. Mom followed, stopping in the doorway to watch for a moment. I didn't say a word. I was angry, but so, so hungry.

THE COAST

THE NEXT DAY WAS bleak. I stayed home all day, only leaving my room every other hour to have a snack. Or a meal.

I didn't bother getting on Facebook. I knew all I would do was check on Tristen's profile. Quite honestly, I didn't have the urge to. The fact was that he liked me. And that was all I needed to know.

Mom stayed away from me all day. The only times we spoke were when she'd let me know food was ready, and I would thank her. Frankly, I didn't have the desire to speak to her either. Things were heated, and I would have preferred to cool down before I said another stupid thing to her. Hurting her feelings was not my intention, and I knew I did just that last night.

I sat in my room for most of the day, studying up for Mrs. Turner's makeup test and reading. I tried to keep my mind off the cat fiasco the best I could, which wasn't that hard when I was eating.

As a matter of fact, the rest of the week seemed to drag on. I met Phoebe in the morning for school and came back home when school was out. We convened at each other's houses throughout the week to work on our college applications, and she continued to give me status reports on every detail of her and Eric's relationship. She was falling hard, and I was happy for her. I decided to give her very little detail about my and Tristen's encounter at the lake, but only because I was afraid of slipping out the gory details of poor little Fluffy's short-lived life.

Tristen and I remained professional at school. We said hello to one another, but secretly gave each other flirty eyes when we did.

He knew just as well as I did that if Sonny found out about our walk to the lake, she would probably spit fire and burn down the whole school.

Whenever I saw the two of them together, I noticed that he was a bit guarded. He didn't hold her hand as much and I didn't see them walking as a pair that often anymore. I did wonder what he was planning to do. He was sweet. He didn't want to hurt her. I was sure he was waiting for the right time to tell her his true feelings.

Mom and I continued not to speak much. The tension melted little by little, but it was still there. She went to work, and I went to school. We ate dinner together and that was that.

Physically, I continued to feel off. I woke up each morning seemingly worse and worse. Or at least I felt that way. The bags under my eyes were still there. My hair was still lifeless. But once I had eaten breakfast, it was as if the cells in my body finally awoke with me to start the day. I noticed that my breakfast and dinner were beginning to seem larger in quantity. My bag for lunch seemed noticeably heavier. My senses continued to heighten once I did have some kind of food in me, but I started to notice I would crave things that I normally wouldn't. Fortunately, the Fluffy incident remained remote, but anytime I would pass an animal—a dog, cat, squirrel, or even a bird—my mouth watered instantly.

I tried to push those insane thoughts out of my brain and continue on with the week. After all, Halloween was quickly approaching.

On Friday, I awoke with the usual sharp, stabbing pain and lifelessness. I made it a point to skip the bathroom routine so that I wouldn't see myself in the mirror. Instead, I dragged myself down the stairs, feeling every step like a mallet to my skull.

I rounded the corner into the kitchen to find my mother sitting at the dining room table with Dr. Walker. This was a surprise.

"Good morning, honey," Mom said with a smile as she stood up from the table.

"Morning," I mumbled.

"Hello, Grace. How are you this morning?" Dr. Walker asked, also with a smile.

What was up with the smiles? Too early in the morning.

"Good. Just hungry," I said. My eyes darted to the breakfast that awaited me. I didn't mean to be impolite, but I couldn't control it.

I sat down. Forgetting anyone was even in the room, I immediately reached out to each plate filled with the breakfast delights. Unfortunately, over the past week, I made a habit of not using utensils. And I didn't care who was watching.

After what seemed to be way too short of time, I finally looked up from my plate. Mom and Dr. Walker were watching intently. Well, this was awkward.

Once I was finished, I sat gazing at all of the empty dishes. Mortified would be the right word for the moment.

"Um...this is a little awkward," I murmured, blood rushing through my face.

"No, dear. You were just hungry," Mom stated.

"Do you feel better?" Dr. Walker asked curiously.

For some reason, I felt the need to be defensive. "Well, of course I do. Wouldn't you if you were starving? If you felt like you hadn't eaten in months and you finally do?"

Mom's expression instantly changed from a smile to a frown. Dr. Walker, however, seemed unfazed.

"You're right, I would. You seemed to look quite lethargic before you had your breakfast. So, are you feeling yourself again?"

"Are you trying to say I looked like shit?"

"Grace!"

"It's okay, Veronica," Dr. Walker said, calming my mother with his hand on hers. "You did look pretty rough."

"Um...thanks?" Was this guy for real? I mean, what was he getting at?

"Honey, how did you feel when you woke up?" Mom asked.

"The same way I always do, Mom. You know how it is. Dull hair, aching stomach, bags, blotchy skin," I said, feeling irritated with the questions. This conversation was beginning to rub me the wrong way. I looked around the room, suddenly feeling the eerie sense of someone else watching me.

"On a scale of one to ten, how would you rate the pain in your stomach?" Dr. Walker asked.

I stared at him for a moment while I tried to comprehend what was going on. He was a doctor. Mom was a doctor. There was obviously something going on with me. And it was obvious that Mom told him every single bit of what had been going on. Including the Fluffy bit. Should I have been worried?

"A hundred and ten," I stated. If he was here teaming up with my mom to find out what was wrong with me, I should be honest.

He glanced at my mom then back to me. Trepidation grew over my mother's face. Dr. Walker didn't seem concerned at all. In fact, I thought I could see a smile beginning to form.

"Grace, what would you say if I told you that I could help you?"

"I would say awesome. What do I need to do?"

"What if we can make you feel better from here on out? What if we can take away your pain and you will stay satisfied for a long, long time?"

"Okay. That sounds great. Is there a pill or something I can take?" Why was he beating around the bush here?

Mom looked down at her hands. She was fidgeting. She never fidgets. I glanced back over at Dr. Walker. "So?"

I knew I must have seemed different. To be quite honest, the constant feeling of being hungry was getting old. I had only finished breakfast minutes ago and could already begin to feel my stomach wanting more. Agitation became frequent and more familiar every day.

"Unfortunately, the treatment I am offering you is not here."

"Okay, so...do I need to go to the hospital for a little while?" I was willing to do that.

"Grace, the only treatment that will fix this is...well...it's only available far away," he explained.

"Far away? How far? New York or something?"

"The facility that carries the treatment used to treat your illness is not in the States," Dr. Walker explained.

"What? What do you mean? Is it in, like...Europe? Mom, is the treatment not legal here?" For some reason, I didn't want to speak to

Dr. Walker anymore. His strange sense of excitement began to show, and I wondered why he would be excited.

Mom seemed to be more distraught. The scared little girl inside me started rearing her tiny head.

"Honey, Dr. Walker specializes in your illness. His facility is on a small island off the coast of Costa Rica." Mom was trying her best to clarify what Dr. Walker just said. She could sense my feelings.

"Costa Rica?" My mind wrapped around the words as they rolled off my tongue. Did I hear her correctly? "Are you serious?"

"We have a state-of-the-art facility that houses over thirty patients with a similar case as you. You will, of course, have your own room, and there are common areas, outdoor activities, and highly qualified professors so that you can continue your education."

I chuckled. "I'm not going to Costa Rica." No way.

"Grace, just please listen to what Dr. Walker has to say," Mom implored, making it quite clear that she was okay with sending me away.

"No!" I yelled, getting up from my seat. "This is crazy! Mom, how can you agree with this? You want to send me away? For how long? And why does it have to be there? Can't you guys fix me here?"

"Unfortunately, our resources are stationed there. Grace, I believe you would really enjoy your stay with us. It's truly like...paradise."

"It's not a vacation! I don't understand. You said there are others like me. What exactly is wrong with me? What is my *illness*?"

Mom stood up from her chair and walked toward the sink. She grabbed a glass and filled it with tap water. I glanced over at Dr. Walker, who was also looking at me. He seemed hesitant.

Before he could begin his explanation, the doorbell chimed. His eyes didn't leave mine.

"Grace, I believe that's Phoebe wondering where you are. You don't have to go to school today if you don't want to," Mom said.

"No, Mom. It's okay. I want to go."

Before I could leave the room, Dr. Walker stood up from his chair and walked toward me. He put both hands on my shoulders.

"Grace, we can help you. I can help you. We will take great care of you. However, you need to make a decision soon. Your condition is declining, and I think you know that."

I looked up at him. His brown eyes pierced into mine. There was a sense of comfort that radiated off his hands, but something deep inside made me feel as though it may not be real.

"Your mother has my number."

I glanced over at my mother. Her face was filled with sadness. There were no tears, but her eyes were crying, and I knew this whole situation was only breaking her heart.

Without another word, I turned and headed to the front door.

"Jeez, lady! We're gonna be late!"

"I'm sorry, Phoebe. Let me just go change and we can get out of here." I tried with everything in me to hide the obvious concern on my face, but she knew better.

She peered over in the kitchen and saw my mother and Dr. Walker.

"Is everything okay?" she whispered.

"Yeah. Everything's fine. That's Mom's old friend. I'll be right back." I headed up stairs and quickly changed.

As we walked to school, my mind wandered. Phoebe was droning on and on in the background, but my thoughts were somewhere between here and the coast of Costa Rica.

Costa Rica? No way. How could I move to Costa Rica? Dr. Walker didn't really explain much either. I mean, I suppose I could have stayed home from school. He was about to give me answers. Answers to why I had been feeling terrible. Why I ate so much. Why I took it upon myself to dine on a poor, tiny cat. Why didn't I stay?

I was afraid. What if I was really sick? Obviously, my body was changing in ways I couldn't understand, but I believe that what frightened me the most was my mind. I had no control over what I felt or did when I was in that "mode." What if I was going crazy? I was a teenager, for God's sake. I should be caring about the *now*. College, boys, parties.

Dealing with an illness took someone who was strong-minded and ready to face reality. I wasn't ready to think like an adult. I wasn't ready to take my life seriously. And I certainly was not ready to leave my best friend and Tristen and my mom.

"You're doing it again," Phoebe said, frustrated. Apparently, we were already at school. "Are you fantasizing about him?"

"No. Sorry, I just have a lot on my mind."

"Well, what are you going to do?"

"Going to do about what?"

Phoebe's expression turned into horror. She dropped her bookbag onto the floor and lifted the back of her hand to my forehead. She was always so dramatic.

I swatted her away. "What?"

"G, didn't you hear anything I just said? Tomorrow is Halloween. And I overheard Sonny talking to her minions about Tristen going to some party she's throwing. She still thinks he'll be with her, which means he probably isn't coming with us."

"What?" I knew this would happen. He chickened out. Another thing added to my already screwed-up day.

The homeroom bell rang.

"I suggest you ask him about it today. For all we know, he just forgot about it."

"I'll ask him."

I'd be so angry if he told me he would come and last minute decided not to. But I refused to let that she-devil win. I needed some kind of normalcy. And Tristen was going to help me get that.

Right before the bell rang for Calculus, I waited by the door to catch Tristen before he walked in. Of course, he was strolling down the hall with Sonny, her minions following close behind. Her eyes caught mine. I quickly turned away. I was so not in the mood for her shit.

As they approached the classroom, her whiny voice rang through my ears.

"So, baby, Mom and Dad are going out tonight to some party. You want to come over and watch a movie?"

He peeked over at me for a millisecond then back to Sonny. "Um, I gotta meet the guys tonight for practice."

"I thought you were off on Fridays," she whined. Ugh, it was giving me a headache.

"Well, I have to go."

She stomped her foot. "Fine."

And I thought Phoebe was dramatic.

When they reached the door to the classroom, she grabbed his face and pulled it to hers. Her mouth opened wide and her long tongue expelled out and into his with full force. Her hands took hold of his hair and pulled. The minions turned the other way. I, on the other hand, couldn't look away. It was like a train wreck. I didn't want to look, but I couldn't help it. It was messy and sloppy, and he tried to back away gently, clearly embarrassed that she was taking it that far.

He finally broke free, lipstick smeared on both their faces.

"That's what you'll be missing," she said as she wiped the little bit of spit left on her face from the violent kiss.

She gave me a fake smile and sashayed down the hall. I held back the bile.

Tristen glanced at me, ashamed. "Sorry you had to see that."

"Well, thankfully I don't have a pencil handy, or else I would have gouged my own eyes out."

He laughed. I loved his laugh. "Thank goodness for that!"

The bell rang. We would just both have to be late for class.

"So, before you go in, I wanted to ask you about tomorrow. Do you still want to go on that double date?"

He began to rub his neck. I hated when he rubbed his neck. He was thinking about Sonny.

"Well, Sonny's expecting me to be at her party."

Son of a bitch.

"Okay, well..." I knew the disappointment was written all over my face. Quite frankly, I didn't care. He told me he would go. Shouldn't I be upset about that?

Somewhere deep down, I just knew this would happen. I didn't finish my sentence. I turned to walk through the door into the classroom and stopped when I felt his hand on my arm.

"No. You know what? Screw it. What time are we going?"

The butterflies in my stomach began their waltz.

"Uh…I'm not sure, but I'll let you know."

I smiled and we both headed into class.

THE DECISION

THE REST OF MY day became much brighter. I informed Phoebe of the addition to our Halloween festivities. She, of course, was over the moon and couldn't wait to notify Eric of our plans.

We discussed our final plans during lunch, which were to meet at my house for seven in the evening and start off with some haunted house hopping. From there, we would visit all of the old, spooky haunted sites New Orleans had to offer, beginning with a visit to Marie Laveau's grave at the Saint Louis Cemetery No. 1 (a woman infamous for voodoo back in her day), Mona Lisa Drive (a very creepy, abandoned road lined with oak trees and Spanish moss), and Hangman's Tree (a tree standing all alone that resembles the face of a slave who was once hung there many years ago). Then, we'd end the evening with an all-night slasher movie fest. All the while, I would have Tristen next to me.

Oh, yeah. This Halloween was going to be the best one yet, and I fully intended on ending the night with a kiss better than what Sonny displayed.

Phoebe made sure to let Tristen in on our plans, for insurance purposes. Sonny was already going to be furious when she found out Tristen wasn't going to be with her for Halloween. All I needed was for her to catch me even looking at him. I wanted to avoid confrontation at all costs and ultimately just leave all of the dirty parts to Tristen.

On my walk home, I rehashed the night Tristen and I took our Walk to Remember. Excluding Fluffy and the vomit scene, I focused on his touch and the way his eyes sparkled as he opened up his deepest thoughts to me. I liked him so much.

I stopped at the corner store to grab a soda before I reached the house. During my search for cash to pay the clerk, I found a tiny piece of paper in my back pocket. I paid the man and continued on with my short walk home, unfolding the yellow Post-It.

Megan 760-555-7589

I had completely forgotten about it. I grabbed my cellphone out of my bag and proceeded to dial Megan's number. I wasn't really sure why I was calling. I knew Mom had some secrets—at least about Dad. But honestly, I didn't have the slightest clue what I was going to say to this person.

"Hi, you've reached Megan. Sorry I couldn't answer, but please leave a message and I'll call you back. Thanks."

I hung up. I already wasn't sure of what I was going to say. I didn't want to leave a mysterious message for the lady. I would just have to call back.

Following the smell of food cooking on our stove, I walked straight into the house and into the kitchen. Mom was setting out the plates. She looked up when I entered the room.

"Hi, Grace. How was school?"

"It was good." I sat down at the dining table, still feeling some tension between us. I wasn't sure when we were going to get past it, but I just wanted to get through the weekend without any input from her.

She brought over the pot and started to pour the roast onto the plate in front of me. The steam rose from the food and the beefy scent found its way into my nose. Of course, without the use of utensils, I buried my fingers into the sauce. It burned, but I didn't care. I continued to dig in.

The food entered my mouth, and without barely a chew, rolled down my throat. As soon as it hit my stomach, I could feel my blood coursing through my veins at a rapid pace. I closed my eyes, because for some reason, I found that if I closed my eyes while I ate, I could taste the food even better. I visualized what it did to my insides. I imagined broken molecules throughout my body, and once the food made its way down, the broken molecules just magically bonded back together. It was mentally satisfying.

After finishing my pot roast, beef short ribs, Mediterranean salad, brown rice, and taco casserole, Mom cleared the plates off the table. With my body replenished, I helped dry the wet dishes.

"So, Gracie, you'll have leftovers in the fridge. And I've prepared some other food for you this weekend."

"This weekend? What's this weekend?" I asked, confused that I'd missed something.

"I have to go to Arizona, dear. Don't you remember?"

With everything that had happened, I completely forgot my mom was going out of town for work. This weekend just took a turn for the better.

I couldn't contain my smile.

"Oh, goodness. What do you have planned?" she asked, concern beginning to show on her face.

"Nothing! Phoebe and I are going to do our usual for Halloween. You know, haunted house hopping and then some bloody movies." I wouldn't dare make it known to her that Tristen and Eric would be with us. I was almost certain she would cancel her weekend—maybe even quit her job—before she let that happen.

She stared at me for a moment, possibly trying to read my face for lies. "I really wish you girls would watch something else other than those horrible movies," she finally said. "They're so grotesque."

"No, they're not. They're fun! Exciting, thrilling, and sometimes even funny."

"Well, just make sure that you eat. Oh, and I already packed some snacks for you. Actually, let me go ahead and put them in your purse now before you forget."

She grabbed what seemed like eight tons of sandwich baggies filled with her homemade goodies and stuffed them into my purse hanging on a dining room chair. Everything from dried fruit, beef jerky, trail mix, pork rinds, candy, and some more beef jerky were stuffed in the bags. Oh, and let's not forget a thermos filled with her amazing pomegranate juice.

"And here's some cash," she added. "This should take care of all the haunted houses. Are you girls coming back here to watch those terrible movies?"

"Yup."

"Okay, well, be sure to text me throughout the weekend. And please, please be careful, Grace. If anything...strange happens, just call me."

"You mean, if I decide to dine on another helpless animal?"

"Grace, it's not a joke," she said sternly.

"Well, it's kind of funny. Remember when I was all, like, 'Mom, I just ate a cat!'"

"Grace Elizabeth! That is enough!" She was getting upset.

"Okay. I was just making light of the situation. Yes, I'll call if anything is wrong."

"That's all I ask. Well, I have to get up early for my flight. I love you, Gracie," she said softly. She took me into a hug, and of course, I hugged back. I supposed I couldn't be mad at her forever. And besides, she was leaving for the weekend, which was amazing. It was like a gift to me from her.

Tristen and I...alone. Well, Phoebe and Eric would be here, but I was sure they'd probably not be anywhere in sight.

As we headed up the stairs together, I stopped her midway.

"Mom, do you think I should go with Dr. Walker?"

She gripped my hands into hers and sighed.

"Grace, I want you to do whatever you want to do. Of course, I don't want you to go. But I believe that it will only help you." She grabbed a piece of my hair and flung it over my shoulder. "I fear that if you don't go, things will only get worse."

"But, how? Mom, what's wrong with me?" I asked with sheer desperation in my tone. "Why do I wake up looking like death and eat like a horse and feed on things with a pulse? Am I some kind of freak? Do I have a disease? Is it going to kill me?"

"Honey, I believe that Dr. Walker should be the one to answer all of your questions because this is what he specializes in."

"But, you're a doctor, too." I didn't understand why she just couldn't explain it all to me.

"I *was* a doctor. Now I'm just an assistant."

I could tell the reality of that stung her heart a little.

This wasn't what I wanted to hear. I wanted her to tell me what to do. As much as I would rather her not do that in other aspects of my life, I wanted her to be straight with me and tell me what to do about this whole situation. Instead, she was giving me some kind of lesson on making my own choices. So not the time.

"I don't know what to do."

"Honey, do what you believe will be best not only for right now, but for your future. Dr. Walker says this is only going to get worse without treatment. But you can change that."

"Why aren't you forcing me to go? It's so...unlike you."

She took a deep breath and put her hand on my back, gesturing for us to continue up the stairs.

"Grace, you're getting older now. I realize that I can't tell you what to do anymore. And it's a big decision to leave your friends, your school, and me. I can't push this on you. I can only support you. Obviously, this is a very serious matter. As much as I want to tie you up and put you on that plane—not now, but *right* now—I just can't do that. If you decide not to go, I'll figure out what we can do to make sure you are healthy. I have done so your whole life. But the decision is ultimately yours."

Still, not what I wanted to hear!

She kissed my forehead. "Goodnight, honey. I'll see you on Monday morning."

And just like that, she closed her bedroom door. I stood on the stair landing, wondering what just happened.

How could she just leave it to me to make what was probably going to be the biggest decision of my life? What would happen if I didn't go? Could I die? But what if I did go? I couldn't just leave my life. The life that I had known for so long. The only life that I knew. How could I live in another place where I wouldn't know anyone else? Where I would be completely alone? Could this be a life or death situation? I mean, we were talking about my health. So, why wasn't she forcing me to go?

Or, why wasn't I just saying yes already? And the worst part was that I had absolutely no idea what was threatening my health. Apparently, something was in my body that wasn't supposed to be there. Or maybe there really wasn't anything wrong with me. Dr. Walker never actually said that I could die from this. He just said it would get worse.

That familiar sharp pain shot through my intestines, followed by a hungry growl. I hunched over and grabbed the banister, as this one was worse than usual.

Yeah, something was definitely wrong with me.

My legs wore me down. The throbbing in my head quickly grew stronger and the rest of my body immediately ached.

On my trudge back to the kitchen, the sound of the waves crashing off the coast of Costa Rica rang through my ears.

I can hear voices, but I can't see anyone. It's dark. Completely dark. I can't see my hands. The smell of salt is in the air. The sound of waves is near. I search, desperately trying to find some sign of light in the distance. Nothing. I don't move forward, afraid of what is ahead. I don't move backward, afraid of what is behind. My body aches. I feel feverish. Frail. The touch of my own skin is rough and rigid. I feel old. Hungry. My stomach is screaming for something. Anything.

Finally, in the distance, two tiny red dots appear. They are close together. They're moving slowly, but closer toward me. I squint to get a better look. My vision is no longer sharp. Only two red dots.

Then, another set appears to the left of them. Now there are four dots. Traveling slowly, but closer. Again, to the right, two more dots. Six red dots. Little by little, but still growing closer. And again, two more dots. And again. And again. Eight, fourteen, twenty—I begin to lose count. They are shuffling in a triangular formation. Their pace is steady. Slow and steady. I brace myself, afraid of what is ahead. The smell of salt is gone and replaced by the smell of rot. It is raw. Real. It is spoiling meat. It is old blood. It is sickly. It creeps into my lungs, causing me to gag.

The dots grow closer and the smell stronger. I hold my breath as long as I can, relieving the odor and preparing for what lies ahead. And then, the first two red dots stop, suddenly revealing a head and a body. A man. A rotting, decaying man. His skin is slipping off his face. His lips are gone. Black ooze drips from both his ears. His clothes are torn. His hair is thin and nearly gone. His fingernails are long. Filthy. And his eyes... His eyes are...familiar.

I stand, quiet. I can't feel my heart. I can't feel anything but hunger.

He cocks his head slightly to one side. His red eyes pierce into mine. They are soft. They are hurt. They are so familiar.

A sense of comfort washes over me. Relief sets in. I know him. I've always known him. It's him. He's there...for me.

His jaw moves as if to speak but breaks off, crashing into the ground like glass smashing into a million pieces.

I reach out to him, grabbing what is left of his hand. His skin is rough and rigid.

"Dad?"

THE CALL

MY EYES POPPED OPEN from my deep sleep. Light barely seeped in through my blinds. I turned my head to look at the clock.

4:30 a.m.

Ugh! I needed to go back to sleep.

I felt a warm wetness on my pillow and assumed I had been sweating from my dream. I reached over to flip on my lamp. The light bulb illuminated my arm, revealing bright red dots. I was bleeding.

There were drops and splotches of blood across my hand and my arm. Panicked, I looked down at my pillow, only to see more blood.

I blinked. My eyes were wet. A tear escaped, landing perfectly on the nail of my index finger. It was blood. The ache in my body began to register in my brain, and I struggled to get out of bed as quickly as I could. When I was finally able to reach the bathroom, I flipped the switch, dreading what I was about to see in the mirror.

Blood, my blood, rolled down my cheeks, reminiscent of tears. The mirror was a blur, but I squinted to focus in on what exactly was going on. I gasped when I realized there was not a single trace of white in my eyes. They were red. Brilliantly red. And blood continued to roll down my face like a running faucet.

From what I could see, everything else was okay. My mouth, my nose, my teeth, my ears. All there. All still intact. I was just crying... blood.

With nausea and hunger beginning to rise in the pit of my stomach, the hunger won, and I knew I needed to make my way to the kitchen. I grabbed a towel from the rack and wiped my face before heading downstairs.

Mom had left breakfast in the fridge and I couldn't even make it to the table. I stood in the refrigerator door to eat.

After allowing the amazing breakfast to settle into my belly, which actually felt like it was all gone as soon as it entered my mouth, I headed back upstairs to get my blood-speckled sheets off the bed and into the wash. I hadn't looked into the mirror yet, but my eyes seemed to have gone back to normal as soon as I began eating.

I chose to once again forget the freaky things happening to my body. It actually became routine to wake up expecting something was going to be wrong.

As I worked to clean my room, thoughts of tonight began to float around in my mind. The butterflies in my stomach commenced their dance as a forecast of Tristen and I together clouded me. I pictured a night full of sexy staring and flirty smiles and tender touches. I pictured a whole lot of almost-kissing moments, which I actually welcomed because when it finally did happen, it would be like opening the gates to heaven. Trumpets and all.

I finally finished cleaning up and decided to shower, still avoiding the mirror. After a towel dry, I wrapped it around my body and sent Phoebe a text to be sure we were all still on track with the plans. Phoebe spoke to Eric. Eric apparently wanted Tristen's number so that he could befriend him and confirm the plans. Finally, Tristen texted me and let me know everything was good to go.

While eating a roast beef po-boy Mom had prepared for me, I started to make my costume.

I dug up some old, ratty clothes and shredded them. With fake blood and silicon flesh left over from a few Halloweens ago, I started to work on my face.

I hesitated but finally looked in the mirror. Everything seemed pretty normal—thank God.

I assessed my eyes, opening them wide and shutting them tight a few times. Nothing there.

It was actually kind of cool that my body was able to heal itself in no time. But I had to remind myself that I was, in fact, sick. There was definitely something wrong with me. As much as I wanted to deny it, my body wasn't allowing me to forget it.

Could my amazing healing abilities be considered a sickness or a blessing?

I wasn't sure, but I had tried my hardest to just forget about all of it. I wanted the night to be perfect.

While enjoying a delicious beef pot pie, I examined my face before digging into my Halloween makeup kit. Some highlighting, black patches, a little prosthetics, and blood should do the trick. I popped season one of *The Walking Dead* into the DVD player—some inspiration—and began the transformation.

Halfway through, my phone rang. I leaned over to glance at the caller ID.

Unknown 760-555-7589

Who the hell was this?

I was about to ignore the call when I realized the number actually looked familiar.

Megan.

"Hello?"

There was no response.

"Hel-lo?"

"Is this...is this Gracie?"

How did she know my name? I didn't leave a message. And Gracie? No one called me Gracie, except Mom.

"Um...yes. This is Grace. Is this Megan?"

"Yes. It's me. How are you?"

Her voice seemed shaky. Almost nervous.

"I'm fine. I, uh...how did you know my name was Grace?"

"Megan?"

"I just knew. I just knew it was you, Gracie."

She sniffled.

"I'm sorry I didn't leave a message. I honestly didn't even know why I called you. It's just that I found your number in my mother's room and figured maybe you knew her."

"Evie? How is she? Is she okay?" Her voice grew frantic.

"Evie? I'm sorry, but I don't know who that is."

"Your mother. My sister."

"Um, my mother's name is Veronica."

"Veronica? No." She sounded confused.

"Megan, I'm sorry, I must have gotten things mixed up. I was calling because I thought...I thought you knew my mother and about...things, I guess. I'm not sure why exactly I called, but I think I may have made a mistake. Thank you for returning my call, though. I really have to go."

"No, wait! Please. Gracie, please. Your mother is Eve. Her real name is Eve."

"Megan, I think you might be mistak—"

"You're from California. Your dad's name is Jack. You had a dog named Lucy. You were very, very sick when you were little."

My heart jumped into my mouth. How did she know those things?

"I'm your aunt, Gracie. Aunt Megan. Please don't hang up. I just want to know where you are. What happened? Why did your mom take you away from us? You got better and she took you away. She never called. She just left." She was clearly crying. Her sadness flowed through the phone.

I didn't know what to say. What could I say to this woman? I had no idea who she was. For all I knew, she could be some psycho stalker. But then again, she could be telling the truth. My mom did have that letter in her closet. She could really be my aunt. My family. Someone my mother hid from me for years.

"Gracie, please talk to me. I have waited to hear from you for over ten years. Are you and your mother okay—"

I hung up.

I didn't know what else to say. She wanted to know so much, but I knew nothing. I didn't even know if she was really telling the truth. Why would my mother lie to me about having a family? We didn't have a family. Mom was an only child. Her parents died in a car accident before she had me. Dad had family, but he was an only child, too. My grandfather died and my grandmother on my dad's side had Alzheimer's and was in a home somewhere far away. There was really no one but Mom and me. Why would she lie about having a sister? What was she holding back?

The doorbell rang.

I knew Mom was keeping things from me, and as much as I wanted to know what the hell was going on, I decided to push those thoughts aside and focus on the now. I wanted tonight to be about me and Tristen.

And as I opened the door, there he was, right in front of me.

"Oh my God! Are you dead?" Tristen asked in horror.

I tried to hold back my smile. He almost looked exactly like me! Blood and dirt smeared over his ratty clothes. Dark circles under his eyes and wounds on his cheeks and neck.

"Oh my God! Are *you* dead?" I mocked.

Tristen lifted his arms out in front of him and stumbled in through the door slowly.

"Brains," he grumbled in a pained voice.

I laughed and panicked at the same time when I realized he was going to crash right into me. I contemplated moving out of the way but decided that standing in his path would probably be quite delightful. Anything to have him close.

I braced myself as he closed in on me. He reached me and wrapped his arms around my body, the butterflies in my belly multiplying in number. His grip was gentle. His touch was tantalizing. I closed my eyes and breathed in his smell. Part cologne, part Halloween makeup.

He squeezed once and pulled away. Way, way too soon. I looked down at my feet before moving aside to let him all the way in.

Don't be shy, Grace.

"So, are you excited about tonight?" he asked as he sat down on the couch.

"Yeah, I'm super excited. It's going to be fun!"

"Is your mom here?"

My nerves were suddenly worse. It had just hit me that we were alone. "Um...no, she had a work thing this weekend."

I couldn't look straight at him. Instead, I headed into the kitchen to get him a bottle of water.

When I walked back into the living room, he was looking at the photo frames on the mantel. "You were super cute when you were little."

"When I was little?"

He turned around and smiled. "Well, of course you're cute now. You are more than cute, Grace."

My face flushed and I handed him the water. He took it with one hand, bringing the other to my face. He traced his thumb over the prosthetic on my cheek. It was soft and slippery from the fake blood.

"This makeup is pretty badass. Where did you learn to do this?"

"Well, I kind of study it."

Confusion crossed his face. "Study it?"

"Yeah. Listen, if you don't know by now that I'm kind of a nerd, well...I guess you're in for a surprise."

Now there was amusement in his eyes. "Tell me. What do you study?"

I turned around and flopped on the couch with a big sigh. Tristen followed, flopping down really close.

"Well, I'm sort of obsessed with horror movies. Zombies mostly. I like to study the makeup and special effects on the actors. Zombies are especially cool because there's really no limit on what you can do. You can make them as gross and bloody as you want."

"So, you like playing with makeup," Tristen stated.

I pushed his chest playfully. "You make it sound like I'm a little kid. It's not just makeup. It's like...art."

"That's actually pretty cool. I like that you like that stuff. Do you practice doing it?" he asked.

"Well, I draw things. How I would like to do the makeup. But I only get to practice putting it on at Halloween."

"Is that what you want to do when you grow up?"

I never actually thought about that. It really wouldn't be a bad idea. I could picture myself on the set of a zombie movie applying makeup to an actor.

"Well, yeah. I do actually."

He smiled wide. "You are one-of-a-kind, Grace Elizabeth Shelley. A one-of-a-kind girl with a weird, gory obsession."

My face flushed and I glanced down at my fidgeting fingers.

His fingers moved in, softly resting on mine to stop them. I looked up into his hazel eyes.

"You don't have to be shy about it. You are. I don't know what it is, but there's something really different about you, Grace."

"In a good way or bad?" I asked.

Chances were that he wasn't going to say in a bad way. It was one of those moments where you just had to hear the answer for validation.

He smiled a crooked smile and tilted his head.

"That's exactly it. You're confident, but not too confident. Some other girl would have said something like 'I know.'" He flipped his hair and pretended to sound like a valley girl.

I giggled. "Someone like Sonny?"

He exhaled, and I could feel his grip loosen. Maybe I shouldn't have asked that.

"You're nothing like her. You're kind of a breath of fresh air."

No one has ever told me that before. A breath of fresh air. I liked it.

The moment grew silent and we stared at each other. It wasn't an uncomfortable, awkward moment or one of those moments where you were trying to figure out how to break it. It was...sweet...calm...a moment that I didn't want to end. I could stare into his hazel eyes all night.

Ding-dong!

Damn it!

I got up and headed for the door. I thought I opened the door to the planet Krypton.

"Hi!"

Tristen stood up to greet Superman and Wonder Woman. To be honest, it was actually quite suitable. Eric was the perfect height and build, and the one black curl over his forehead completed the costume. And Phoebe...well let's just say her top half was certainly a wonder. She filled out that costume in more ways than Wonder Woman ever could.

"Wow! You guys look amazing! Like the real deal!"

"Thanks! And you two look awesome! G, you guys so match," she said with a wink. I laughed nervously, hoping Tristen didn't catch that. I was sure he knew how I felt about him by now, but I didn't want him to know that he was the topic of most of my conversations with Phoebe.

I gestured the two members of the Justice League in and we stood around the living room.

"You guys want something to drink?" I asked, suddenly feeling pretty parched myself.

It was then that I noticed Phoebe had been hiding something behind her back, under her red cape. Her scarlet lips formed into an O as she swung her arm around to reveal a large bottle of Southern Comfort liqueur, also known as SoCo.

"Oh, yeah?" Tristen asked as he rubbed his hands together. Eric nodded his head in approval.

I felt a little anxiety coming on but tried to hide it with a smile.

"Oh, come on. Don't clam up on me now."

I gave her a look. "Phoebe, can I talk to you in the kitchen? We'll be back, guys."

I linked my arm to hers and we walked over to the kitchen.

"Grace, what's wrong?" she asked as she began her search for some drink glasses in my cabinets.

"Phoebe, I don't think we should drink."

"Why not? It's Halloween! Our favorite night of the year!"

"Shh! Listen, we're going to be driving and I just don't think it's a great idea is all."

"But we always have a couple of drinks. We sneak your mom's wine, like, every year."

"Yeah, but we were home when we did that. Just watching movies. Can't we wait till we get back?" I asked. We had never secretly drunk alcohol and drove around town before.

I was trying my hardest not to be a buzzkill, but Phoebe's face proved that I was unsuccessful. She stepped away from the drink-making and grabbed both my shoulders as if she were about to shake some sense into me.

"Grace, it'll be okay. Eric and I talked about it, and he's only going to have one drink. He's driving tonight so that we can all drink and have a good time," she reassured me. Phoebe knew me, and she knew I was a little more conservative than she was.

I took a deep breath in and caved. She figured as much and hugged me. "We're going to have an amazing time, G. This is your night to shine for Tristen."

"Yeah, but what if I get stupid drunk or something?" I began to panic at the thought. Tristen just told me that I was one-of-a-kind. Getting wasted and stupid might change his mind. I didn't want to be like the rest of his friends, including Sonny.

Phoebe headed back to mixing drinks. "G, this isn't your first time drinking. Just limit yourself."

Her stupid matter-of-fact face came back. Ugh! She was right, and I agreed to at least have one drink.

Phoebe grabbed two glasses and I followed with the other two. Tristen and Eric were standing near the couches, talking football.

"Okay, guys! Here you go." I handed a glass to Tristen.

"Thank you," he said softly and smiled.

Phoebe held her glass up and we all followed. "Here's to a great night ahead of us! Happy Halloweenie!"

We clinked our glasses and took a swig. Kind of strong, but the fruity, spicy taste of whiskey hit the spot. Phoebe and Eric kissed after their clink, and Tristen and I smiled and glanced down at our glasses. Our moment would come. Soon.

THE HOUSE

WE FINISHED OUR GLASSES of SoCo and Coke—one glass for me and Eric, two for Tristen, one and a half for Phoebe—and headed out the door. Eric's old black Mustang shimmered in the moonlight and Tristen sighed.

"Now *this* is a car!"

"Yeah, dude. It's my baby."

"Hey!" Phoebe shouted.

"You know you're my baby. But she's my baby, too." He cupped her face and kissed her forehead gently before opening the car door for her. Phoebe smiled sweetly and giggled. Yeah, those two were definitely in love. My heart filled with happiness for both her and Eric, but a twinge of jealously followed.

I glanced over at Tristen. He watched them, too, with a smile growing bigger and bigger. He switched his gaze to me, and I melted once again.

He was a romantic. I could tell.

We piled into Marilyn, as Eric called his car, and began our fun-filled night.

Our first stop was a haunted house that had been named one of *The Travel Channel*'s Most Extreme Haunted Houses in America. Phoebe and I went there almost every year since we could remember, and while there were some scenes that were quite graphic and demonic in nature, it was still one of the best places I'd been to. I had almost peed my pants walking through it. And if I actually ever did, it would totally be worth it.

We pulled up to the parking lot and, of course, the line was almost down the street.

We waited and watched a rock band play on stage and became judges of our own little costume contest as people danced all around us. Phoebe pulled out her flask of SoCo and she, Tristen, and I took turns sipping. As we continued to near the entrance, a recognizable feeling washed over me. I suddenly remembered that I hadn't eaten in some time.

When I went to reach for my purse for a quick snack, I realized that I'd left it in the backseat of Marilyn.

Tristen noticed and touched my arm.

"Hey, you okay?" he asked.

"Yeah, I'm fine. I just realized I left my purse in Eric's car."

"Did you need some money? I can buy you something to eat if you're hungry." He seemed concerned...and to have read my mind.

"No, it's okay. I have money. But, yeah, let's go grab something to eat really quick before we get inside," I said, eager now to put something into my mouth. I knew where this would lead if I didn't. And I wasn't going to let anything ruin the night, including my ridiculous urges to eat unsuspecting house pets.

I informed Phoebe and Eric of our plan to grab a quick bite before we headed over to the row of food booths.

"What are you in the mood for?"

I quickly read over my options. Hot dogs, corn dogs, nachos, and beer. Of course, my stomach craved all of the above, but my mind thought there's no way I was going to eat like a Hungry Hippo in front of Tristen.

"Are you hungry?" I asked. His answer could affect my choice. If he chose to eat, it could take all eyes off me and allow me to eat a little more.

"Yeah, I can eat. I'll get whatever you get. Your call."

Great. At least he was being a gentleman and allowing me to choose.

"Um...let's do hot dogs."

"Okay, two hot dogs coming up."

I wished it was three hot dogs. All for me.

"Here." I reached in my back pocket for a twenty.

"Grace, are you trying to make me look bad?" he asked playfully as he took my twenty out of my hand.

"No, not at all. I can pay for my own things, you know."

Tristen folded the twenty and reached around my body. As he reached down and stuffed it back into my back pocket, my heart pounded so loudly in my ears that I couldn't even hear the band playing in the background anymore.

"Keep it. Dinner's on me," he said. His voice was low and sexy. All I could do was nod as he took my hand and led me to the hot dog booth.

He ordered two hot dogs and a large Sprite. My mouth began to water as the smell of cooked meat swirled around my head.

"Cheers." We tapped our hot dogs together and each took a bite.

I had never really eaten outside of what Mom cooked for me every day. Why would I? There was constantly food in our house. Every once in a while, I would grab something extra during lunch or maybe grab some fries at the food court in the mall. Honestly, it never really hit the spot compared to Mom's home cooking. But Mom was completely against any fast food. She'd say that it was unhealthy and that she would rather die a thousand deaths before she'd ever bring it home for dinner. A little dramatic if you asked me, but I got her point.

It was insulting to her if I would ask for something outside of what she cooked. We would sometimes order take-out from a few fancy restaurants around town that Mom did approve of, but she wouldn't dare allow us to eat it without adding a little something extra herself.

This hot dog, however, was pretty delicious. But it really wasn't doing anything for me. After the last bite, my stomach growled for more. I decided to ignore it and wait until we could get back to Marilyn. I'd be able to get into my purse and munch on the snacks Mom made for me.

We made it back to our spots in line just before we reached the entrance. Eric and Phoebe were in front of us. Eric wrapped his arms around Phoebe's waist.

Tristen looked over at them, and then at me.

"You gonna be okay?" he asked into my ear.

I shivered when I felt his warm breath. "Yeah. You?"

"I'm a little scared," he admitted.

"Really? Do you need me to hold your hand?" I teased.

"No! But I think you'll grab mine at some point."

"Oh, yeah? You don't think I can handle this?"

"No. I don't. I think you're gonna scream."

That was an insult.

"What?" I asked, playfully but serious.

"You heard me. I think you're scared."

"Well, we'll see who's scared when we get in there."

"I'll be right behind you. Watching your every move," he threatened.

I shrugged my shoulders and smiled. "Okay, but you're gonna be disappointed."

He smiled back as we entered one of the most extreme haunted houses in America. Smoke immediately clouded our vision as we walked into strobe lights and darkness. A bloody-faced creature jumped out of the wall within the first two seconds, prompting Phoebe to jump, which in turn caused Eric to squeeze her tighter. He was such a sucker.

We walked slowly in a single-file line through scenes of a graveyard, a bloodied operating room, and a room filled with fake body parts hanging on chains. Screams erupted from the girls ahead of us. Vampires, Michael Myers, and deformed monsters jumped out at us from all sides. The smell of the smoke machines and Halloween makeup permeated the air. I smiled at this, remembering just why I loved Halloween.

Occasionally, the line would slow down and we would come to a halt. Seeing as the space was quite small, we waited, breathing down the person's neck in front of us until the line sped up again. Normally this would make me a little uneasy. But Tristen was behind me.

He leaned down to whisper in my ear. "You scared yet?"

My neck tingled and I smiled. The lack of light and the sense that we were practically alone—since no one was paying attention to us—gave me a boost of confidence. I turned my head to look him in the eyes. We were so close at this point that all I had to do was pucker up and his lips would be on mine. The smell of his clean cologne filled my head.

I gave him my sexiest smile and he returned it. I suddenly felt his hand, slowly intertwining his fingers with mine. My breath caught and I became completely lost in the moment. My heart pounded under my shirt when I realized this could finally be it. Our first kiss.

His other hand reached up to caress my arm, slowly sliding up and down. I allowed myself to fall back a little into his chest as I prepare for the moment I'd been waiting years for. He held me up with his body, strong and firm.

As I counted to three in my head and closed my eyes, I heard the man behind him.

"Hey dude! Line's moving!"

Tristen turned around. "Oh, sorry."

Oh, damn it to hell!

Right at that moment, my stomach growled again, and a pain shot through me. I instantly hunched over, swallowing the yell that wanted to escape my throat. Tristen grabbed hold of my waist and hunched over with me.

"Grace? You okay?" he asked, concern in his voice.

I inhaled deeply and focused on his touch instead.

The man behind us yelled again. "Hey, dude, can you please walk ahead? Y'all are holding us back!"

Tristen turned around quickly. "Hey, DUDE! Chill okay? Give us a minute!"

I grabbed on to his jeans and tugged, hoping that he understood that I was trying to tell him to calm down. He turned around immediately.

The pain escalated, and I knew I couldn't stand up straight just yet. I peeked over to my right and noticed an exit door. I grabbed

Tristen's leg again, fighting to move my way closer to it. Then, Tristen swooped me up effortlessly into his arms and we moved out of the line. Eric and Phoebe were ways ahead of us, and I knew they would wait at the end till we got out.

He carried me through the door and found a curb to sit on. He never let me go. I buried my face in his neck and began to pray for this horrible pain to subside.

"Grace, tell me what's wrong. Does your stomach hurt? Do you need some medicine? Tell me what you need." His voice was soft and full of genuine worry. I was in so much pain but mortified at how this must have looked.

Oh my God! I was the girl who passed out in the haunted house because she couldn't take it!

At least, that was probably what people were thinking as they walked by.

I finally managed to say something between my stabbing pains. "I need Marilyn."

"You need Marilyn? Grace, I don't know—"

"My purse."

"You need to get to the car?" He caught on quickly. "Got it."

Within an instant, Tristen was up and power-walking with me in his arms toward the end of the haunted house to meet Phoebe and Eric. Just as I thought, they were waiting and sucking face, of course.

"Hey, we need to get to the car. Now," Tristen huffed.

Eric pulled his keys out of his pocket and bolted for the car. Phoebe, Tristen, and I quickly followed.

"Gracie, what's wrong?" Phoebe asked, worry filling her voice. I knew she was concerned—she never called me Gracie.

I couldn't talk.

"I don't know what happened. She just collapsed in there so I got her out as fast as I could."

"There's blood on your neck, Tristen. Is that fake or Grace's blood?" she asked, panic creeping through her voice. Phoebe turned my face away from his neck to get a better view.

"Shit! Gracie, your nose is gushing!"

I reached up slowly to see what she was talking out.

"What?" was all I managed to ask before everything went black.

THE PARTY

"GRACE? GRACE. PLEASE WAKE up. Can you hear me, sweetheart?"

My eyes fluttered open and horror flushed over me when I saw a man covered in blood and gore hovering in my view. Was I having one of my morbid dreams? I sucked in a breath of air and flinched a little, slowly realizing that I was not dreaming and that Tristen's beautiful face was underneath the Halloween makeup.

"What happened?" I asked.

"You passed out. How do you feel?" he asked, rubbing a cold wet cloth on my forehead. I turned my head, taking in the coolness— apparent then that I was lying down in the backseat of Marilyn.

My mouth was dry. As I imagined a cold glass of water, Tristen brought a bottle of water to my mouth, slowly spilling a little at a time into it. How did he know what to do and when to do it all the time?

I heard Phoebe's voice. "Is she awake?"

"Yeah, she's awake. Grace, tell me what you need."

I reached around in search of my bag. I knew exactly what I needed. It was the only thing on my mind.

Of course, Tristen sensed this and handed me my purse. I reached in and grabbed one of the Ziploc bags of treats Mom made for me. I began to eat, feeling a thousand times better before I even swallowed, and a million times better knowing Tristen was right next to me.

"Oh, she's fine. Thank God." Phoebe said in relief.

"How do you know, babe?" Eric asked curiously.

"Because if she doesn't eat," she said, turning to give me the stink eye, "she gets faint and sick."

I managed to give her the finger in between bites.

"Is that true? Do you get sick if you don't eat?" Tristen asked. I nodded, only wanting everyone to just stay quiet and let me eat.

Tristen smoothed my hair out of my face. His expression remained the same, still and serious. Concerned. Phoebe continued to give me the stink eye. Over the past few weeks, she had also noticed changes in me. She didn't quite know to what extreme my body had been changing, but she had noticed that there was a change in my eating habits. I explained to her at some point that Mom had been monitoring me to make sure that everything was okay. She naively believed the whole hormones story and never really asked any more questions as to why I had been eating so much.

She did, however, witness me become extremely fatigued and sickly when I needed food one day while we were studying at my house. It was very hard not to pig out in front of her, but I managed to get by without seeming like a hungry maniac. Luckily, I was able to come up with an excuse to end our study session early so that she could leave, and I could devour as much food as humanly possible.

"You scared me," he whispered.

"I'm sorry."

"Don't talk. Eat. Now, woman!" His gorgeous smile grew, as did mine.

Marilyn rumbled beneath us and the vibration kind of felt good on my achy body.

"G, are you feeling okay enough to continue our night?" Phoebe asked.

Throwing the third empty Ziploc back into my bag and reaching for another, I mumbled yes. To be completely honest, what I really wanted to do was take Tristen back home to my house and prepare a lovely dinner for just the both of us. But seeing as how I'd been fighting with everything in me to keep from swallowing down my treats whole—plastic baggie and all—that didn't seem to be a good idea.

I managed to sit up straight and concentrate on eating like a lady. Tristen kept his hand on my leg, glancing over at me every ten seconds to make sure I was okay.

"Are you feeling better?" he asked.

"I'm fine. Sorry about what happened back there." I looked down at my fingers and began to fidget. Tristen squeezed my thigh, prompting me to look up at him.

"Grace, you never have to be sorry for anything when you're with me."

"But I made a complete ass out of both of us."

"No, you didn't. Not me, anyway."

I stared at him, stunned that he would say that. His smile radiated off his face. I remained still, until a second later when I couldn't hold in my laughter any longer. We both laughed out loud, causing Phoebe to turn around.

"Hey, what's so funny?"

"Nothing," we sang in unison.

"Okay, so what are the plans? Mona Lisa Drive? Or do you guys want to head to Mardi Gras World for some more haunted house action? Minus the passing out and nosebleeds, of course." Phoebe chuckled.

I plucked the back of her head.

"Ouch! That hurt!"

"Do you guys want to crash a party?" Tristen asked.

"What party?" Eric asked, intrigued.

"Sonny's party."

I shot a look at Tristen, not quite sure what to think.

Phoebe spoke for me. "Sonny's party? Why the hell would we go to that witch's house? She and her minions are probably getting ready to jump on their broomsticks to fly around town and wreak havoc on innocent children."

"To crash it," Tristen answered. "And I kind of have some things to talk to her about," he whispered only loud enough for my ears to hear.

He glanced over at me, and the butterflies fluttered around in my stomach as if they were trapped and trying to get out. What was he suggesting? Was he suggesting we go to Sonny's party so that he could tell her once and for all that he wants me? Why now?

Holy crap!

"I'm in," Eric declared. He looked over at Phoebe, who was now watching me, searching my eyes for any hint to the answer she was supposed to give. I was completely stumped, not sure of what or how to feel.

"Is that okay with you, Grace?" Tristen asked, resting his hands on mine.

I stared into his hazel eyes, frantically searching for an answer in them. They were soft, and despite his bloody dead-like makeup, there was no mistaking the language between us in that moment. He wanted me to say yes.

"Yes," I caved.

"Well, all right. Let's go crash a party!" Eric hollered.

"Really, Eric? Is it that exciting?" Phoebe asked, sarcasm dripping from every word.

"Come on, babe. You know it'll be fun. Plus, I'm pretty hot. You can rub it in her face." Eric smiled a glamorous smile as he threw his arm around her shoulder and pulled her closer to him in the bench seat.

Tristen kept his eyes on me. He leaned in closer. "Are you sure?"

"I was going to ask you the same thing."

"I've never been more sure of anything. I was actually going to break up with her really soon. I should have done it a long time ago. And Grace, you're smart, beautiful, funny, and everything I have wanted for a long time. Sonny is pretty and all, but we just don't go together anymore."

"But you don't even know me that well, Tristen," I stated, suddenly feeling insecure.

"I know enough to know that I want to know more. And I can't get to know you more with...baggage."

"Yeah, but don't you think—"

He put a finger over my mouth as if to shut me up, but gently. I did as he implied, desperately hoping that he would switch his finger out for his lips.

Instead, he placed his palms on both sides of my face and tenderly squeezed.

"It'll be okay. There'll be tons of people there. We can just walk in, I'll pull her aside and tell her, and she won't even know you're there. Honestly, she'll probably already have another boyfriend by the end of her party."

He knew that I was nervous. He was trying to reassure me that everything would be okay.

I nodded, hoping that he was right. This had drama written all over it, but I had Tristen, Phoebe, and Eric on my side. If Sonny tried anything stupid, Phoebe would be on her like white on rice. And something told me Eric wouldn't pull her off this time.

Tristen directed Eric to Sonny's house from the backseat. As we pulled up, I soon realized that it wasn't a house at all but a mansion nestled away in a quiet cul-de-sac. The street was lined with cars and the enormous yard was infested with drunken teenagers. We found a spot almost around the corner and made our way up the street to the party.

The house sat between two slightly smaller houses, both dark as if the neighbors weren't home. It was two stories and white, with four round pillars acting as if to hold up the roof. It was reminiscent of the White House, and I briefly wondered what the hell her parents did to afford such an amazing home.

We walked up to the lawn, which was larger than it looked from the car. The long driveway led to a circular one. In the middle stood a huge water fountain that reminded me of photos in history class of the old water fountains in Rome, only this one had a large *W* visible through the sparkling water. The initial for *Westwood*, I assumed. Or maybe it was the first initial for *Wow-I've-got-a-lot-of-money*. Why did I suddenly feel the need to hashtag that?

Teenagers were scattered around, some holding cups of what I presumed to be alcohol. The bass pumped inside the house, sounding muffled from the outside. There was absolutely nothing Halloween about this party. No one was dressed up. No one had Halloween makeup on. This sort of pissed me off—like they were too good for it. No one was too good for Halloween.

As we walked up the driveway, eyes began to descend upon us. Of course, since no one here was in costume, we were the oddballs. Eric grabbed Phoebe's hand, probably preparing himself to hold her back as we approached a group of girls who began giggling and pointing their fingers at us. I didn't look their way, trying hard not to give them what they wanted, which was attention.

Tristen's hand also found mine, and I looked down to make sure it was really happening and not just something I was imagining. I glanced up at him, only to find him smiling down at me, lips stretched from ear to ear.

This was amazing and scary at the same time. I was thrilled to be this close to Tristen and that he was going out of his way to make a big gesture but also scared out of my mind that tonight would end up badly. Hopefully, the inside of this castle would be filled with preppy drunks, allowing me to keep away from Sonny and her minions. I was sure my zombie-like appearance would help hide me, too.

As we made our way to the line to get in the front door, the music got louder, along with the sounds of drunken teens. My heart began pounding. And then...my stomach growled.

Oh, not now!

I did eat three and a half bags of treats, but I didn't know what I was thinking when I thought that would be enough.

I tried to ignore it, concentrating on hiding from you know who.

Upon entering the house, I felt like I was suddenly in the middle of Bourbon Street on Mardi Gras day. We could barely maneuver through the crowd. Tristen kept a hold of my hand as he led the way. Phoebe clutched onto my shirt, making sure not to lose me through the crowd. People were drinking, talking, and partying all around us.

From the little glimpses I managed to get in between the sea of people, the inside of the house was just as immaculate as the outside. There were two large majestic staircases, one on either side of the foyer. Everything was white, and the walls were filled with hanging portraits of artwork. I would not have been surprised if somewhere in this house there was a bathroom made out of twenty-four karat gold. It screamed, "I'm rich, and I can do anything I want."

I began wondering where Tristen was taking me until suddenly, I felt a shift around us. We moved into a tiny opening in one of the rooms. Everyone around us were moving, bouncing and swaying to the loud music.

A hip-hop song slowly turned into a more dance-friendly song. I recognized it immediately and thought about how much I loved it.

Tristen stopped in front of me, bopping his head to the rhythm as the rest of his body began to follow. He turned around to face me and leaned in close to my ear.

"I love this song!"

I smiled wide, knowing full well that we would have the same taste in music.

His arms found their way around my waist and he pulled me closer. Without taking his eyes off mine, he moved me to the music with him, and I was forced to let go of any inhibitions I had.

His beautiful zombie face lit up when I began to carry his same rhythm, and we were soon in sync. I wrapped my arms around his neck, suddenly forgetting about Sonny, food, or what tonight may bring. Thoughts of my mother, my body changing, Megan, and my possible departure to Costa Rica began trailing off into a distant area of my brain. I could feel the bass pumping between us, and I allowed my body to relax in his arms, feeling safe and sound, just what Capital Cities was singing about.

A bubble began to form around Tristen and me, and soon it felt as though we were the only people in the room. He lifted his hand and caressed my neck. The touch of his skin created sheer bliss, jubilation that made my body quiver. The alcohol from earlier in the night still coursed through my veins, generating a slight buzz. I closed my eyes and tilted my head up, giving him more space to rub and send tingles through me.

I felt a soft kiss on my neck, causing my eyes to roll. His other hand met my face and he gently forced me to look into his smoldering eyes. Our bodies continued to move together, swaying and bopping in the same motion, as if it were meant to. He grazed his thumb over my bottom lip and gave me a half-smile. I wasn't anticipating it. I wasn't bracing myself. I didn't even begin my countdown. In that moment, the only thing I wanted more than anything was to taste his lips on mine. And as we continued moving to the music, I leaned in.

As soon as my lips touched his, I felt his body relax, as if it were a relief. My body did the same, and without a skip to our beat, we pressed our lips harder onto one another's. His hands moved from my face and through my hair as I pulled him closer to me, feeling as if he weren't close enough. His lips parted, as did mine, and his tongue slowly and tenderly entered my mouth. The butterflies in my stomach danced with us and my heart slowed its beats. Without catching a breath, we kissed slowly and passionately, savoring every moment. I grabbed the back of his head, gently pulling his hair. We kissed like we had never kissed anyone else before. There was nothing else in the world that could be better than what I was feeling.

Suddenly, I felt a force on my back. Someone pushed me firmly against Tristen and he quickly held on to me, stopping us both from falling to the ground. I turned around feeling really pissed off that someone ruined the incredible electricity that was flowing between us—maybe a little punch-drunk from it being our amazing first kiss.

Sonny was standing in front of us, arms folded across her chest. The music suddenly stopped. Kind of like what happens in the movies when the DJ stops a track too quickly and it screeches. I stifled a chuckle at the resemblance.

"What the hell, Tristen!"

THE APPETIZER

I GLANCED AROUND AND noticed that we were suddenly in the middle of a large crowd, resembling a crowd watching a dance-off or something of that nature. Phoebe and Eric stood on the opposite side of Tristen and me. Eric had his hands around Phoebe's waist, and I swore I could see his muscles flexing as if to be holding her back.

Tristen stepped in front of me and quickly tried to defuse the situation.

"Sonny, can we talk in private, please?" he asked in a calm manner.

"No! No, we can't. What the hell are you doing here with her? And why the hell are you two making out in my house?"

"Sonny, you really want to do this right here, in front of everyone?"

"I don't give a shit who's around! You obviously have no trouble making out with that skank in front of everyone here."

She actually had a point. I briefly began to realize that it did take a lot of...balls...for Tristen to come here in front of all his friends with me. To be fair, though, he did plan to break up with his girlfriend.

"So...what? Are you two going out now? When the hell were you going to tell me this?" she asked.

I suddenly felt pity for her having to find out this way. I looked down at my feet, awkwardness and shame beginning to seep through me.

"Sonny, I'm sorry. I didn't want it to go down like this. That kiss just kind of happened. I was coming to tell you that..."

He looked over at me. Feeling everyone's eyes begin to rest on me, I started to wish there was a rock I could crawl under.

"What?" she asked impatiently.

Tristen turned back to Sonny. "I was coming to tell you that we can't be together anymore. I have feelings for Grace." He turned back toward me, and I swore I could see a twinkle in his eyes.

I had known for a couple of weeks now that Tristen was interested. But I guess it didn't completely hit me until then. Hearing him actually profess this was something completely different. It was a clarification. It was the truth. It was the beginning of something wonderful. It was Tristen holding his heart in his hands, and it was mine for the taking.

Phoebe smiled across from me, and I knew that she was thinking the same thing.

I shifted my eyes to Sonny, who was now turning into a monster right in front of us. She threw her tightened fists to her sides and yelled, "Are you freaking kidding me?" She pointed at me. "How could you possibly want to be with that? She's a waste of air, Tristen. She's hideous!"

"Hey!" Tristen yelled. "I know you're mad. And I'm sorry." He grabbed my hand. "I came and said what I had to say. We're through, Sonny. We're leaving."

Tristen began to lead us through the crowd. As we walked past Sonny, she grabbed a handful of my hair and pulled me to the ground. I lost Tristen's hold on the way down. I grabbed the back of my head immediately, wondering to myself if this was really happening. Tristen quickly ran to my side, and I caught a glimpse of Eric holding Phoebe back. There was no doubt if he let her go, she would come fight Sonny for me. I ignored Tristen's hand, as suddenly a wave of anger flowed through me.

This was definitely an *Oh no she didn't* moment.

I got up slowly, watching Sonny's every move.

"All right, Sonny. What do you want to do? You want to fight over Tristen or not? Because either way, he made his decision. And it was me."

"You're nothing but trash, Grace Shelley. You always have been. And sooner or later, Tristen is going to realize that," she said as she pushed my shoulder.

I paused and straightened up. "Sonny, if you touch me again, you will regret it." The tone in my voice surprised me. I was not sure where it came from, but it was from somewhere deep in my suddenly starving stomach.

The usual hunger pain shot through me and my anger only seemed to have progressed. I realized then that I was famished.

"What are you gonna do, Granny-panty? You gonna beat my ass?" she mocked.

I sized her up, waiting on her to make the first move. I hated confrontation, but something inside me was beginning to change. I was becoming more and more angry. And hungry. I was angry because I was so hungry. Her miniskirt and tank top began to piss me off. Her strawberry blonde hair pissed me off. Her sky-high heels and long tanned legs were just pissing me off!

"Well, do something!" she yelled, shoving my shoulder again. Before she could move her hand away from me, I grabbed her wrist in one quick motion and twisted. She instantly bent down in pain. I didn't let up. I twisted more and more as her body became rigid. I would have even twisted more, but she grabbed my hair with her free hand, pulling as hard as she could. I winced and let go of her.

I managed to pull away from her grip and jostled her to the side. Before I knew it, she ran and jumped in the air, landing on me and causing us both to tumble onto the ground. She straddled my body and began to throw punches and slaps at the same time. I held my arms up over my face, blocking her.

"Sonny!" I could hear Tristen's yell and see him run over to us. He attempted to pull her off me. Everyone around us screamed, "Fight! Fight! Fight!"

She clutched onto my hair again before Tristen finally grabbed a good hold on her and pulled her off. Only, she would not let go of my hair. This was a huge problem. My hair was precious to me. No one had ever tried to pull my hair off my head, and I certainly was not going to let it happen tonight.

As Tristen continued to pull, so did Sonny. I had every intention of slugging her right in the jaw, but that changed the second her arm grazed my mouth. The scent of her skin reached my olfactory receptors. Ever since the moment I tasted raw meat and poor Fluffy, the coppery raw scent of flesh and blood flashed through my mind, and I could suddenly smell it.

I had to have it. I wanted it. I needed it.

Without a second thought, I opened my mouth and clamped down onto Sonny's arm. A horrifying scream escaped her throat as I bit down harder, allowing the blood to pool in my mouth.

Oh, the sweet blood.

I instantly drank it down, only wanting more. I bit down even harder, feeling her skin begin to tear. Her scream intensified into a louder and more pained shriek. Her body became limp, and Tristen halted his attempt to pull her off. But I couldn't stop. I needed to taste the raw meat. My stomach growled harshly, roaring as if to tell me not to stop. I pulled harder and harder with my teeth, twisting my head in the process to get a better grip to rip and tear.

Finally, with one last tug, a large piece of her fleshy tissue pulled away from the bone. I felt her tendons dangling from my chin as I chewed on her fresh meat. Some of the tendons were stubborn and wouldn't disconnect from her body. I grabbed a hold of them and rip them away with my fingers, shoving what was left into my mouth as if it were spaghetti.

I could no longer hear her screams. All I could do was close my eyes and savor the taste of her raw flesh and succulent blood in my mouth. I chewed frantically, hoping to swallow it quickly and get back to the rest of her.

But when I opened my eyes, she was no longer there. Sonny was farther away from me now. I looked around. Everyone stood still, not uttering a word. I glanced at Phoebe, her hands covering her mouth in disbelief. Eric's expression was unreadable, as if he was completely flabbergasted at what was happening, his face white as a ghost. I scanned the crowd for Tristen. He was standing farther away now, too, with Sonny hunched over at his feet. He, too, had a look of shock and disbelief.

Remorse immediately flooded me, as I began to come back down to Earth and feel like I slightly quenched my thirst and craving.

What did I do? What was everyone thinking?

After what felt like an eternity of sheer silence, Sonny's minions ran over to help her. I managed to stand up and begin to make my way through the crowd. As I power-walked toward the front door, people backed away slowly, making a clearance for me to get through. I was pretty certain no one wanted to get close to me.

"Grace!"

Tristen called out my name, but I didn't stop. What the hell could he possibly want? I needed to get away. I needed to get out of this house and away from everyone.

I picked up the pace, finding myself panicking before I finally reached the front door. I swung it open and ran out into the fresh air. No one was out on the lawn or driveway, probably because they were all watching the real-life zombie movie take place inside.

I wasn't sure where I wanted to go, but it had to be anywhere but Sonny's house.

Reaching the end of the driveway, I turned and headed down the street, away from where Marilyn was parked. I doubted Phoebe and Eric wanted to have anything to do with me after what they'd just witnessed.

I ran to the next block and stopped when I reached the beginning of a walking trail that looked like it led to a small neighborhood park. Struggling to catch a breath, I took a seat on the street curb and panted.

After about ten minutes, I heard Tristen's voice again and his running footsteps. As soon as he spotted me, he rushed over.

"Grace! Are you okay?" he asked between catches of breath.

"No! I'm not okay! Tristen, didn't you see what happened back there?" I asked, trying to hold back my tears.

"Yeah, I saw. You defended yourself."

"What? You call that defending myself? I bit her, Tristen! I bit her arm!"

"I know. I saw. And, yeah, biting her might have been a little overboard but she started the fight. I know her. Sonny's ruthless. She probably wouldn't have ended that fight until she knew that she hurt you."

I stood up and began pacing, pushing my hair out of my face. Words started spewing out of my mouth. "The raw meat was one thing. The cat was a different story. But this...this is bad."

"What? Raw meat? Cat? Grace, what are you talking about?" Tristen asked, confusion in his tone.

I stopped and faced him. I threw my arms in the air and could no longer hold back the tears. "I ate a cat! I ate a freaking cat, Tristen!"

I wasn't exactly sure why I felt the need to reveal this fact. But in that moment, I was scared. What I had just done to Sonny would be equivalent to having stabbed her with a knife. Except, the knife was in the shape of my teeth.

Tristen's expression had bewilderment written all over it. I was almost certain he was wondering if what I had just said was that I'd eaten a cat. Or maybe he was wondering if I'd said I had beaten a mat. Surely, whatever he was thinking had to suggest to him that I was a psycho maniac.

The silence between us was deafening.

"Well, say something," I demanded.

Tristen slowly walked toward me. I exhaled deeply and looked away, knowing damn sure that this was going to be the beginning of the end.

When he reached me, he grabbed my hand and lifted it up to his chest.

"Grace, did you just say that you ate a cat?"

Shame of that night skulked through me.

"Grace, listen to me," he said as he gently grabbed my chin and swiveled my head in his direction.

What could he possibly say?

"I don't care."

"You don't care?" I asked in disbelief.

"No, I don't care. Well, obviously, I do care. You just told me you ate a cat. I mean, I guess that's kind of...weird. And I'm sure you're going to explain it to me. You did just bite my ex-girlfriend's arm and eat her flesh. I'm not even going to pretend that's not crazy. But she's going to be fine. We called an ambulance and she's got all her friends there with her. It's just her arm."

But I bit it. I knew I bit a huge chunk right off.

"Grace, I like you a lot. There is something about you."

"Yeah, something completely insane!" I exclaimed.

Tristen shook his head. "No. Something...unique and different. I can't quite put my finger on it, but I like it. You're so different than everyone else. Than Sonny. You don't care about what you wear. You don't have a bunch of mindless girls following your every move, waiting patiently for you to tell them what to do. You're you. You sit at the lake and think about things. You study hard and strive to do well in school. You watch horror movies and appreciate things that no one cares about anymore, like Halloween. I'm sure you can tell me something new about yourself and I will love it. Right now. Tell me."

"Um..." It was hard to concentrate on things that I liked at that moment. My focus was on how amazing Sonny's arm tasted. "I...uh...I like comic books?" That came out as a question because, honestly, I wasn't sure if it was what Tristen wanted to hear.

"See, you like comic books! That's awesome. So do I! Tell me something else," he said, eagerly awaiting my response like a kid waiting to receive a popsicle from his mom.

"I...I like to watch cartoons right before I take a nap," I confessed with a sudden need to explain this revelation. "It puts me to sleep," I mumbled.

Tristen chuckled and his smile grew wide. "You see, I love that about you. Grace, whatever's happening, I want in. I want to help and listen and go through it with you."

I pulled my hand away from his chest, briefly wishing I wouldn't have done that because I could no longer feel his heart beating. Not to mention, his solid chest on my fingertips. From what I could feel, he had to be hiding something good under his shirt.

"Tristen, you don't understand."

"Then tell me, Grace. Tell me and I will."

"It's complicated."

"Well, start with the cat. So, you ate a cat? What, like did your mom accidentally run over it and you guys decided to cook it for dinner?" That should have sounded like sarcasm, but his facial expression was serious and seemed as though he was truly trying to understand. "I mean, that would be weird and gross, but there had to be some kind of legitimate reason."

"No!" I said in frustration.

"Then what? What happened?"

"I ate it! I saw it when I walked home from the mall. I killed it with my bare hands. And I ate it. Right there. Completely raw."

His face changed. There was no expression now. I turned away from him, mortified at what I had just revealed. Certainly, he was done. I would guarantee that the moment I turned to face him again, he wouldn't be there anymore.

But I continued, hoping that I wasn't speaking to the air.

"Something's wrong with me, Tristen. Something terrible. I can't explain it. I'm hungry all the time. I just want to eat. My mouth waters at the thought of anything going into it. I wake up every morning feeling awful. I'm tired and weak and so hungry all the time. But the second I eat, I feel better. I don't know why I ate that cat, but it was the best thing I have ever eaten. Until tonight. When I tasted Sonny's blood, something inside me wanted more. I was just so...hungry!"

I held back the urge to cry my eyes out. I cherished the moment, as it was the first time I was able to finally tell someone other than my mother what I was going through. A weight lifted off my shoulders, and I suddenly felt like I could breathe at last.

I felt Tristen's hand on my shoulder. I closed my eyes, thanking God that he didn't run away.

He pulled me around to face him. "Grace, you're right. Something is wrong. I don't understand why you have this urge. It's weird and scary. But whatever it is, we'll figure it out. I want to help you figure it out."

"Why? Why isn't this making you run for the hills?" New Orleans didn't have hills really—it was pretty flat—but I had always wanted to use that expression.

Before Tristen could answer, the sound of sirens in the distance interrupted. I couldn't tell if they were police or an ambulance, but terror began to course its way through me.

A second later, I see Phoebe and Eric running down the street in our direction. Behind them, drunken teenagers began scattering about, spewing out of Sonny's enormous palace.

My panic intensified as I recalled seeing Phoebe's expression after I'd eaten a piece of Sonny's arm. I knew the best friend I once had would be too terrified of me to keep that title.

I braced myself as Phoebe and Eric approached us, but relief washed over me when she ran straight into me with open arms. She hugged me tight, almost as if she hadn't seen me in decades.

"Gracie! Are you okay?" she asked as she pulled away and assessed my face.

I nodded. It was all I could do while I fought back the tears from the thought of our precious friendship ending because of my stupid actions.

"Guys, the cops are there. We really need to get out of here," said Eric.

Phoebe grabbed my shoulders and stepped back to get a better look at me. She knew in an instant what I was thinking.

"G, we need to get you out of here. Sonny's going to rat you out, and the cops are going to want to take you away."

"Was it that bad?" I asked, worry and panic deepening into my nerves.

"Let's just say that Sonny will probably never be able to use her arm again, if she's even able to keep it," Eric stated.

I glanced over at Tristen. Judging by the shocked look on his face, he didn't realize her injury was that bad.

"Oh my God! Oh my God! What do I do?" I asked, desperately hoping someone could give me an answer.

Phoebe shook me once. "Grace, there's no time to think about what happened. We need to get you far away from here."

Phoebe handed me off to Tristen and we ran toward the car.

As we headed back, the ambulance was already parked at the house and Sonny came out of the front door lying on a gurney.

Thankfully, everyone was too busy watching Sonny being wheeled into the ambulance to notice us. We managed to get back to Marilyn without anyone stopping us.

We piled in and drove off down the street.

My heart was racing a million miles a minute. My thoughts were scattered.

Okay, Grace, step back and get the bigger picture. What happened?

Well, Tristen and I kissed. We kissed and danced, and it was incredible. It was sweet and passionate and everything I thought it would be. His lips were soft, his touch was tender.

And then Sonny caught us. She pushed me. I warned her. She pulled my hair. And I bit her. And it tasted remarkable. Fluffy had nothing on what Sonny Westwood tasted like. It was bitter and sweet. It was moist and warm. It was succulent and better than anything I could ever imagine eating in my life. Her fleshy tissue melted in my mouth. And the texture of her raw meat was supple and really reminded me of Mom's beef stew, only more flavorful.

I closed my eyes and thought of the moment I tasted this, suddenly feeling the craving for more.

"Grace, are you okay?" Tristen asked, interrupting my train of thought.

I glanced over at him and nodded. I peeked at the rearview mirror and saw Eric's eyes switching between me and the road. Phoebe turned to me as if to say something but refrained for the moment. I felt the awkwardness in the air and decided someone had to say something.

"I'm sorry."

I could feel Tristen's eyes on me, but he didn't say anything. Now that he knew how bad Sonny's injury was, could he be regretting his decision to stay with me?

"Grace, you don't have to be sorry. That bitch deserved it," Phoebe added.

"Well, you have to admit...it was pretty harsh," Eric chimed in.

Phoebe whipped her head toward Eric. "Eric, she did what she had to do. Sonny wouldn't let go of her."

"Yeah, babe, but she nearly bit her arm clear off. How in the world could anyone even do that? Man, she must have some seriously strong teeth."

I knew at least one person in our group would protest to what I did. Phoebe was my best friend, and although I briefly thought that our friendship would end because of my actions, deep inside I knew she would defend me. But I still wasn't sure what Tristen was thinking.

And just as I'd decided that he was beginning to hate me, he grabbed my hand and squeezed. "Dude, you never know what your body can do when it's in survival mode."

"Yeah, but then she...ate it," Eric said in disgust.

Everyone grew silent. I looked down at Tristen's hand as I opened mine and interlaced our fingers.

"Grace, why did you eat it?" Phoebe asked.

I glanced up at her. Her eyes were filled with concern and genuine curiosity. I knew she was as scared as I was. But would anyone in this car understand that Sonny's smell was so enticing that I just couldn't resist? That I had no other option but to taste her? That my mind wouldn't allow me to do anything else?

"I...I don't know. It just...it smelled so...I just wanted to taste it. I don't know, Phoebe. It just tasted so good," I admitted.

"What did it taste like?" Tristen asked, intrigued.

I didn't look at him. "It tasted sweet. And soft. And really, really good."

Everyone grew silent again. I assumed they were letting it all seep in. It wasn't everyday someone would talk about what human flesh tasted like.

"Where are we going?" I asked, hoping to change the subject. Part of me wanted to go home so that I could eat something Mom had left over. I was pretty hungry.

"We're going back to my place. We can't take Grace home because if the cops want to ask questions, that's probably the first place they'll go," Eric answered.

I sunk back in my seat, realizing that he hadn't spoken directly to me since we drove away from Sonny's house. He was growing skeptical of me.

THE COUCH

THE REST OF THE ride was silent. Tristen kept hold of my hand. Phoebe, who normally had no issues ever speaking, remained speechless. I could see the tension in her shoulders the whole ride.

We pulled up to an apartment complex with a sign out front that read *Coldwater Creek*. We were about twenty minutes from my house. Seeing as no one really knew Eric at the party since he didn't attend our school, this was probably the safest place to be.

We unloaded out of the car and headed up the stairs. Once on the third floor, Eric unlocked his door and let us in.

It was a tiny apartment with the usual drab eggshell-colored walls and beige carpets. There was a small couch in the living room, with a glass coffee table between it and the TV. An Xbox console rested on the floor with discs scattered around it. To the right was the kitchen. A refrigerator that seemed like it could only hold eggs and a carton of milk stood in the corner, and next to it was a stove that only had two burners. Past the kitchen and living room was a door that I assumed led to the single bedroom and bathroom. This must have been what they called a bachelor pad, seeing as there were a couple of empty beer bottles lying around and no type of interior design. It seemed like this was just the place he slept and hung out with his buddies, playing video games on occasion.

Phoebe's kind of guy.

We walked in, and Eric went straight to the fridge to fetch some beers. I assumed he felt like he needed a drink now. After what I did tonight, I was feeling the need for one myself.

"So, what's the plan?" Tristen asked, opening the beer Eric handed him.

Phoebe came out of the bedroom; she had changed into shorts and a tank top. She seemed comfortable in Eric's home.

"Well," she said, "I think we should hang out here for a bit and just chill till everything dies down."

"Phoebe, it's not just going to go away. Grace hurt Sonny pretty badly. The cops aren't just going to quit looking for her," Eric stated.

"Can you please stop talking about me like I'm not here?" I asked, beginning to feel really irritated with how he was treating me.

Eric didn't say anything. I walked over to where Tristen sat on the couch and plopped down next to him.

"Yeah, babe, it's rude," Phoebe whispered in his direction.

"I agree that we need to figure out a better plan," Tristen said. "I mean, we can always say that it was self-defense. Grace was defending herself."

"Yeah, but how many people actually saw her eat Sonny's arm? That's got to be something...illegal, right?" Phoebe asked, running her fingers through my hair. I loved it when she comforted me.

"I don't know, but either way, you know Sonny's parents have a ton of money and they're going to make sure Grace pays for what she did." Eric had a point, but I rolled my eyes. He was still not speaking directly to me.

"Well, for now, why don't we just stay here for the night? If that's okay with Eric." Tristen looked at Eric, who shrugged as if he didn't care, then back at me. "I know you're freaked out right now. Why don't we just get some sleep, and when we wake up in the morning, we'll figure it out."

"I like that plan," Phoebe said, yawning.

Eric remained quiet. I felt his skepticism, and I was sure that he was questioning even having me in his home. But, honestly, I didn't think he would protest because I was Phoebe's best friend and he knew for certain that she would not be okay with kicking me out to the curb.

"I'm gonna get you guys some sheets and pillows. The couch doesn't pull out, but you can try to fit on it together," Phoebe said.

"The floor will be fine." I blushed. The thought of Tristen and me being that close to one another sounded amazing and terrifying at the same time.

Phoebe came back out of the bedroom with sheets, some pillows, and a change of clothes for me and set them down on the couch. I stared at my emotionally tired friend, wondering just what she was thinking about.

She glanced over and smiled before coming to sit next to me. Tristen got up and asked Eric to show him where the bathroom was. He was giving Phoebe and me a moment alone, and I appreciated that very much.

"Phoebe, I'm so sorry I ruined tonight. Halloween, our special night."

"Are you kidding me, G? You kicked some Sonny ass!"

"No, I didn't. I practically chewed her arm off!" I said, feeling the remorse set in again.

Phoebe's expression changed into a serious one. "Grace, why did you do it? Why did you eat it? Why didn't you spit it out?"

I couldn't look her in the eyes. Shame overpowered me. "I don't know. It just happened."

"I can't help but feel like you're not telling me something. I want you to know, Grace, that you can tell me anything. I'll never judge you. You're my best friend till the end. We're soul buddies, remember?"

The moment Phoebe and I claimed this title flashed through my memories. We were about eight or nine years old and playing with Barbies at my house. Phoebe was Barbie and I was Ken. I remember our Barbies got into an imaginary fight and I began to cry because I told her that I thought Barbie and Ken were soul mates and shouldn't fight. Phoebe looked over at me and said that *we* were soul mates. We were soul buddies. And from then on, we were.

I smiled at that beautiful memory. "Tomorrow, I'll explain everything I know about what is going on. Tonight, let's just get some sleep. You look really tired."

She lifted her arms above her head and yawned. "I am...and still pretty tipsy. Don't be surprised if you hear some mysterious noises coming from the bedroom," she said and gave me a wink. "I'm not that tired yet. I'm going to have me a few more swigs of our SoCo and make my man happy!"

I noticed a slither of blood on her leg about a finger-length long when she moved to stand up. "Hey, what happened to your leg?"

"Oh, I think I hit it on something in the haunted house."

She examined it and touched it gently, removing some of the blood which revealed a narrow cut in her skin. "Don't worry, Eric will kiss it better," she said with a devilish grin.

I shook my head. She walked over to the bedroom door just as Tristen entered the living room.

"And we'll talk about that one tomorrow, too," she said and nodded in Tristen's direction.

The blood rushed to my cheeks. "You know it."

"I love you, Grace."

"I love you, too, Phoebe."

She shut the door behind her, and I stifled back my tears. Tristen sat beside me on the couch and placed his hand on my thigh.

"You okay?" he asked.

"Yeah. I'm fine," I lied. "Can I ask you a question?"

He nodded.

"Why are you on my side? You and Sonny were together for a while and I hurt her pretty badly. Aren't you upset about what I did?"

"Sonny has everyone on her side. I mean, I'm worried about her, but I'm worried about you, too. I don't think you would have done that if there wasn't something wrong with you. And I honestly think Sonny will be okay."

I bit my bottom lip and hoped that he was right. "Are you ready to go to sleep?"

"Sure, I'm a little tired."

A pang of pain shot across my belly. I remembered my Ziplocs and reached down into my purse to grab a few bags. Feeling a little self-conscious after what happened just a couple of hours ago, I decided to ask Tristen if he was okay with me eating.

"Do you mind?" I asked, lifting my bag into the air.

"No, go ahead. Are you hungry?"

"Starving."

He got up and began laying out the sheets and pillows on the floor. "So, what is it that you're eating, anyway?"

"Um, it's just treats my mom makes. There's some beef jerky and dried cranberries and other stuff. Do you want one?" I asked, trying to be polite but secretly hoping he wouldn't take the offer.

"Sure, I'll take some beef jerky. I'm kind of starved myself."

I handed him a slice. He bit down and began to chew.

"So, your mom makes all this herself?"

"Yeah, she makes pretty much everything we eat. She's an amazing cook. Oh, duh. You would know because you ate some of it."

His eyebrows furrowed. He held the beef jerky up to his face and began to analyze it.

"What's wrong, you don't like it?" I asked. How could he not? It was marvelous!

"It just doesn't taste like any other jerky I've had. What kind of meat is this, do you know?"

I reached down into my purse to grab another baggie. "Um, I'm not sure actually. Mom never wants me around when she's cooking. I actually don't know any of her recipes."

"Huh," he mumbled and ate the rest of the jerky.

I walked over to the sink in the kitchen and started to wash the Halloween makeup off my face. If I woke up in the morning with this stuff on, I was sure I would really look like a zombie.

After drying my face with a hand towel, I turned to find Tristen taking his shirt off. My reaction was to quickly turn back around.

"Oh, I'm sorry. I didn't know you were—"

"It's okay, Grace. Do you mind if I sleep without it? It's got fake blood and crap all over it."

"No, no. I don't mind." Of course I didn't mind.

I turned around toward him and struggled to keep my jaw from hitting the floor. Just as I suspected, his six-pack abs and perfectly sculpted chest were revealed. I watched his muscles flex as he reached down to take his shoes off, and when he stood back up, I took in the contour of his stomach. My eyes scanned his body, leading down to his jeans.

I took a deep breath and headed toward our makeshift bed. Only, there was one on the floor and one on the couch.

"I figured maybe you'd be more comfortable on the couch," he explained when he noticed my confusion.

"Oh, thank you."

Damn it. He was being polite. Not that I expected anything to transpire between us intimately, but I had hoped to be close to him.

"Do you mind if I take off my shirt?" I asked, realizing then how ridiculous that sounded.

His cheeks flushed and he smiled. "Um...sure?"

"No, I have a tank top on underneath. Don't think it will be that easy, Miles."

"I didn't think it would be, Shelley."

Tristen turned around, being the gentleman that he was, as I took my shirt off and changed into the spare shorts Phoebe handed me before heading off to bed.

I hopped over his sheets on the floor, careful not to mess it up. I stretched out on the couch and watched him reach over to the floor lamp and switch it off. The room was completely dark now, which was disappointing because I could no longer see his beautiful body.

We were positioned like a capital T, with me on the couch and him on the floor. I turned on my back, wondering what was going through his mind.

"You have a tattoo," I stated.

"I do."

"What is it?"

"It's a phoenix. I got it when my grandpa passed away."

I knew it. His grandpa. His impact.

He continued. "He was awesome. The most loving and caring person you would ever meet. He was smart. He was funny. He was everything I wanted to be."

"What happened?" I asked curiously. I didn't want to pry and hoped that he was okay with me asking him this question.

Without hesitation, he answered. "He got sick. Lung cancer."

"I'm so sorry, Tristen." It hurt me deeply to know that this was painful for him. I had never lost anyone in my life. I didn't know my father well enough to have lost him when he left. The emotions he felt right now were foreign to me, and I could only imagine what it was like.

"It's okay. He died when I was thirteen. It was tough because he was like a second dad to me, you know. No one would even tell me he was sick. They were afraid of how I would react. But they finally did, and I was able to cherish every moment I had left with him."

"Phoenix. Isn't that a symbol of strength?"

"Yeah. He had gotten sick and fought it for some time. He'd been through a lot in his life. He was a Marine and had been to Vietnam. Got shot and discharged. His wife, my grandmother, died before I was born. He had just been through so much and still managed to see the brighter side of things. He was a phoenix. Always rising from the ashes."

My eyes swelled as I listened to Tristen. His voice was full of grief, and I knew exactly why his grandfather impacted his life. An envious emotion shot through me when I realized I didn't have anyone in my life like that.

"It sounds like he was really important to you," I said.

"He was. I thought about him a lot tonight. It was a little scary, what you did to Sonny, but I think my grandpa would have understood why you did it. Or, he would have at least tried to understand."

I would have really liked his grandpa.

It was quiet for a few moments and I wished I could be beside him, holding him.

"Grace?"

"Yeah?"

"What do you think is wrong? Do you think you're sick?"

I sighed. "I don't know. I don't know what is happening to me."

"Are you scared?"

"Very."

Before I knew it, Tristen stood up from his makeshift bed on the floor and lay down next to me on the couch. I slid over as much as I could to make room, but the couch wasn't very wide at all, forcing us to be as close to each other as we possibly could be.

He turned me toward his chest, and I unconsciously nestled my head into it. His skin was warm, and I could feel every muscle in his unbelievable chest. He wrapped his arms around my body and our legs intertwined together. He kissed my forehead and held me tight.

I didn't know what made me do it, but a floodgate seemed to open, and I cried and cried into his chest for what seemed like hours. He didn't say a word. Just held me tight. Never letting go. He kissed my head every time he felt me cry harder.

I realized that I hadn't actually shown any emotion since this began happening to me. I was too busy wondering what was wrong and worrying about my next meal and hiding it from the people I loved, like Phoebe, to truly take in what was happening.

Something terrible was going on, and I had no idea what it was. It was a feeling of the unknown and complete loneliness. I felt like I was the only person in the world experiencing it. There was a big decision to be made soon, and I was the only one who could make it. And I had no clue what to do.

Hearing Tristen's heartbeat against my ear was what slowed down my crying until finally, there were only sniffles. I looked up at him, curious to see if he'd fallen asleep.

"Do you feel better?" he asked, gazing into my eyes.

His thumb slowly grazed my cheek, wiping away the last of my tears. I nodded, and before I knew it, our lips were touching.

He tightened his grip around my body as his soft lips pressed against mine. It was long and sweet, followed by smaller, shorter kisses. Slowly, he turned his body and lifted himself. He hovered over me, and I bent a knee to make room, allowing his leg to fall in between mine. Holding his body up with one arm, as if to not put too much pressure on me, he smoothed the hair out of my face with his free hand and stared into my eyes.

"Grace, you are so beautiful," he breathed.

"How can you say that? I'm not nearly as perfect as Sonny," I stated.

"Are you kidding me? You're far more perfect than Sonny. She hides behind a pound of makeup and expensive clothes."

"Yeah, but you like that."

"No, Grace. I like you. I've always liked you."

"You what?"

"You heard me. I have always liked you, Grace."

"Since when?"

"Since my first day at Middleton. Sophomore year. You were walking into art class and I was already at my desk. Your hair wasn't this long. It was right at your shoulders." He chuckled. "You had the cutest little look on your face, like you were nervous about our first day of school."

I remembered that day as if it were yesterday. It was the first day I saw Tristen. The first day I knew I wanted to be with him.

"The first day of school is always so nerve-racking. Why didn't you talk to me?"

"Because you intimidated me."

Oh, come on. He had to be joking.

"I was intimidating?" I asked, surprised.

"Well, yeah. You had already been there a full year before me. And you were so adorable. I was this scrawny little dude and you had this big, beautiful hair and those tiny freckles around your nose. I didn't know what to say to you," he admitted.

"Wow. That is pretty unbelievable, Miles."

"Well, you better believe it, Shelley. By the way, I like this last-name calling. It's sexy." He grinned a devious grin. I sunk into the couch as my breathing grew heavier.

I smiled the sexiest I could and whispered his last name. "Miles."

This obviously worked because before I knew it, his lips were on mine again and with more force. He relaxed his arm a bit, allowing his body to press against mine. His tongue entered my mouth and found mine, and they began their dance. There was a sense of urgency in our kiss, but our bodies didn't match. We maneuvered to each other's movements, slowly finding a perfect rhythm. His hand reached down to my leg, lifting up my thigh and slowly caressing my skin all the way up to my stomach. He didn't move under my shirt. Instead, he reached for my face and stroked my cheek with the back of his fingers.

I melted further and further into him with every touch. I let my hands roam free on his bare back, tracing my fingernails up and down the curves of his muscles.

The notion of sex was always in the back of my mind when I thought of Tristen and me. I was almost certain that he was no stranger to it. He and Sonny were together for some time, and it only seemed natural for them to explore and become intimate. Not to mention, something told me that Sonny was the promiscuous type.

But let's face it: I was a hormonal teenager with a sexy guy stretched out on top of her in the dark.

My mind drifted off to places I had never explored, and my body moved in ways it never had while Tristen kissed me. There was no sense of anxiety or nervousness as I pondered on the possibility that this may very well be the last moments of purity for me.

But as we continued kissing under the moonlight seeping through the blinds of the one window in the room, I realized that Tristen was going no further.

I wanted it, but I began to get the suspicious feeling he wasn't on the same page.

I pulled away from our kiss, catching a breath and looking into his eyes. His were still closed, as if he were continuing to be in a state of bliss.

He finally opened his eyes. "Are you okay?"

"Are you?" I asked, curious to know why he was holding back. Honestly, I wasn't completely sure I was on board. But after everything I had been experiencing, maybe it wouldn't be a bad thing. Who knew what tomorrow would bring, or if this would be my only opportunity to share my first time in ecstasy with someone? And there was no one else I would rather share it with.

"I'm more than okay, Grace. I have you in my arms. I'm kissing you. God, you're such a great kisser. I can kiss you for days."

"Is that all you want to do?" I asked bravely, bracing myself for his answer.

He sat up, resting on his heels, and pulled me up with him. "Grace, are you insisting we have sex right now?"

I looked down at my hands and began to fidget.

Great. Maybe I *was* that easy.

He pulled my chin up with his finger. "Trust me, I do want to. But not here. Not now."

"Why?"

"Because Phoebe and Eric are in the other room. Because of everything that happened tonight. Because I want it to be romantic and at a time when we're hoping the cops won't come and smash down the door searching for you."

"But what if they do? What if I get into trouble and they take me away?" I asked, suddenly realizing that could very well happen. Not only the cops taking me away, but Dr. Walker taking me away to Costa Rica.

Panic crept up through me when I recognized that this could be the last moments I had with Tristen.

"That won't happen. I won't let it. We'll figure it out, Grace. I just got you, I'm not letting you go that easy. I know this is new and it's so crazy to feel this way so soon, but I've liked you for too long. I'll run with you."

"I feel like this is a dream. Like you aren't really here right now," I admitted.

"Well, I am. And I'm not going anywhere."

My heart began to sing a love song when I heard those last words. It was as real as it would get. Tristen was finally here and not just in my thoughts. The truth was that he always wanted to be here. With me. And I couldn't be happier.

He hugged me tight before planting a small kiss on my lips.

He pulled me down to the couch with him, and I rested in his arms, quietly listening to his heartbeat. We didn't speak, and soon sleepiness overpowered everything else. I drifted off into a slumber with thoughts of Tristen and me frolicking on the beach of an island... somewhere off the coast of Costa Rica.

THE DREAM

MY EYES POP OPEN. I can't see anything. I can't move. I feel a weight on my back, but I'm not sure what it is. The only thing I'm sure of is the striking hunger in my stomach. I feel my veins throbbing through my skin as my heart pumps, and the nauseating feeling of emptiness washes over me.

I'm starving. My mouth is dry, and I can't think of anything else but the taste of human flesh. I stand up, struggling to keep my balance and fighting against the weight of my own body pulling me down to the floor.

I want to eat. I need to eat.

There is a smell. There's a smell familiar to me in the air. I can taste it. I can almost see it in the darkness of the room.

It calls to me, a small voice inside my head. I see the smell and it gestures for me to follow it.

I listen. Slowly and eagerly, I allow my body to follow. I imagine what the end of this trail has to offer. I envision a delicatessen of sweet blood and mounds of flesh. My mouth begins to water.

I open a door into darkness. I hear or see nothing, but the scent grows stronger. The smell leads me to something. Something soft. Something warm. I kneel down next to it, closing my eyes and taking in the heavenly familiar aroma.

My heart begins to race as I stroke the soft, warm object that is now at the level of my waist. Whatever it is, it seems to be in a parallel position.

I take in a deep whiff from point to point, hearing my stomach howl at me to begin my feast.

I glide my hand slowly against the object, allowing the warmth to seep through my cool fingertips. I bring my nose down, inhaling one more large breath before I finally open my mouth wide and sink my teeth in.

Tepid liquid quickly begins to pool around my lips. I suck it up and bite down deeper, making my way through the layers. With each one, I dig deeper with my teeth, gnawing through, eagerly awaiting the moment I taste what I have been yearning for.

But before I can make it there, I hear a screech and the object begins to move. It's moving. It's trying to get away from me.

It can't. It is mine.

I hold it down, using all of my strength, as I search around with my free hand in the darkness. I feel something. Soft, feathery... almost like a cloud. I grab it and quickly lay it over the source of where the moans are coming from.

The object tries to push my arms away, but I fight it. I have to protect what is mine.

I press down hard using both my hands. The object continues to try to maneuver its way out of my hold, but I use every ounce of force I have to keep it still.

Then finally, it stops. I leave the cloud where it is and search for the spot I was working on. I find it and slowly place my finger inside of what I have already started.

Using my nails, I begin to tear. I open wider, using my other hand to scoop out what I was looking for this whole time.

And with the first taste, my mind flies off to a faraway land. A land that is familiar to me, but so foreign. A place that I have only dreamed of.

Each taste, each mouthful awakens a part of me that I have never known. The sweet and bitter tenderness of every chew sends my body into a whirlwind.

The sound of a car alarm in the distance resonates into my eardrum. The pitter-patter of cockroach legs on the tree outside clatter my senses.

My eyes begin to adjust to the darkness, and I am finally able to see all the red that surrounds me. The odor of what lay before me intensifies as I dig deeper and deeper into it.

I climb on top of the object, tearing and ripping deeper into it. I cup the fatty substance into my palms and pour it into my mouth. I feel every molecule in my body strengthen.

I find a cavity, an opening as I tear my way upward. I excavate deeper and deeper, until I have no place else to go.

I am ravenous. It is what I have longed for. It is what I need.

"Holy shit!"

I looked up to see Eric standing at the threshold between the bathroom and his bedroom. A towel was wrapped around his waist.

"Holy shit! Holy shit!" His eyes were lost in what he was looking at.

Tristen frantically entered the room.

Eric turned away as Tristen and I turned to one another and locked eyes.

"Grace?" I could see the fear in his face as he assessed what was all around me. I looked down with him.

What have I done?

I brought my bloody hands up to my face. Fleshy tissue and stringy tendons dangled from my fingertips. Through my fingers, I saw the 'object' that I was straddling.

I'm not dreaming?

A hollowed-out torso lay beneath me. Veins and skin and copious amounts of blood covered the entire upper portion of the body. I glanced up above the chest area, allowing my eyes to follow up the neck and to the pillow that rested on the head.

I began to shake my head in disbelief, suddenly realizing that what I thought was a dream was actually real.

"Grace, what happened?" I heard Tristen ask.

I didn't look at him. The breasts of the lifeless body were exposed, leading me to recognize that the only people in the room were Eric, Tristen, and myself.

Where is Phoebe?

I looked over at Tristen. His eyes were bulging. I glanced at Eric, who was now kneeling down against the wall with his head in his hands. Loud sobs were escaping his throat, making it clear that he was crying in fear and loss.

"Grace, talk to me," Tristen encouraged.

Eric shot up from his position. "What the hell are you doing?" he yelled.

"Grace, please say something."

"She just...she just killed my girlfriend!"

"Grace, just keep your eyes on me." Tristen held a hand out, gesturing for me to come to him.

"Dude, what the hell are you doing?" Eric shouted and clutched onto Tristen's arm.

Tristen turned his body in a fluid motion, gripping Eric's hand in his. Eric was quite a bit taller than Tristen, and much more robust, but Tristen's confidence seemed to make him look stronger.

"What the hell are you doing, Tristen? We need to call the cops!"

"Eric, calm down! I know this shit is crazy, but we can't call the cops, all right?"

"Are you kidding me?" Eric barked. "I leave my girlfriend sleeping in the bed to take a shower and I come back to her dead... torn-up body. I'm calling the damn cops!"

"No! This shit is unreal, man. But Grace is sick. She didn't mean to do this. We need to help her."

Eric glared at me. Tears continued to roll down his face. He pulled his hand away from Tristen's grip and turned the other way. Tristen brought his attention back to me.

I had not moved an inch since the light had come on. Afraid to look anywhere else, I kept my eyes on Tristen's, searching desperately for some proof that this was real and not a dream.

"Grace, I'm going to get you some water. Maybe it'll help you come back down to Earth, okay? I'll be right back."

I couldn't find any power in my body to respond. Instead, I watched him leave the room and fought the urge to lift the pillow to get one more look at my soul buddy.

From the corner of my eye, I saw Eric pacing the room and whimpering under his breath. I was afraid to look at him.

Grace, what have you done? You killed your best friend. You murdered someone. And the worst part is, you aren't doing anything. You aren't crying. You aren't moving. You aren't—

Eric's hands were suddenly around my throat. He lifted me up and threw me down to the floor.

I struggled to catch a breath, opening my mouth wide and hoping some air would find its way in. His large thumbs pressed down harshly onto my esophagus. Terror flowed through me when I realized that he could kill me that very second, but I didn't fight him off. Instead, my arms stayed limp on either side of my body. My mind wandered, and I realized that I was welcoming the moment. I wanted to die. I wanted this life to be over.

My mother's smile flashed through my mind. Sounds of her cooking in the kitchen rang through my ears. The aroma of her floral perfume enveloped me in a goodnight hug. I watched the moon outside my window, longing to see my father again. I imagined the features in his face and wondered if I looked like him now. The doorbell chimed, and I opened the door to my dear, dear friend Phoebe. Her long, soft hair bounced around her face as she playfully laughed, and the sound of her sweet voice hummed through my many memories of us.

A single tear fell from my eye. And then...I could breathe again.

I stared at the ceiling, coughing and inhaling deeply to catch my breath. I felt a hand on my face.

"Grace, are you okay?"

I opened my eyes and there he was.

"Come on, Grace. We have to get out of here now!"

Tristen threw a bloody baseball bat to the side, and with one single motion, pulled me off the floor. His hands were sweaty and shaky.

"Don't look at anything but me. Okay?"

"What did you do?" I asked. Something seemed terribly wrong.

"He...he was hurting you. I had to do something."

Tristen's eyes were bugged. He looked like he could have been high on drugs. High and spooked. "Tristen, is he dead?"

"Grace, we have to go."

"Tristen! Is he dead?" I asked. Panic and anxiety were beginning to rear their heads. I knew what I had done. But what had Tristen done?

"Grace, he was trying to kill you. I hit him with a bat. He wouldn't get off of you. Now, let's go!"

I peeked over to where Eric was sprawled out on the floor. I had to check. I had to see if he was dead for my peace of mind.

I knelt down next to his body, noticing the large, bloody dent in his head. I assessed it briefly. It seemed as though his head took several blows, all in the same spot. I searched for the carotid artery on his neck—something my mother had taught me one day because I was curious to know. I found it and lightly rested two fingers on it.

There was no pulse.

I looked up at Tristen, who instantly read my mind. Without another word, we headed toward the front door.

Before leaving the bedroom, I glanced over at the bed one last time.

My friend. I'm so sorry. I love you, Phoebe.

I fought the urge to run back into the room. Tristen grabbed the keys to Marilyn off the coffee table and we hurried out of the apartment.

"Where are we going?" I asked. I had no idea what we were going to do.

"I don't know. But we need to get far away from here," Tristen stated. He seemed to be in mission mode.

Tristen drove us out of the parking lot and away from the apartment complex. There was complete silence as we drove aimlessly down the street. Thoughts of the events leading to that moment circled my mind. But I couldn't help but notice the amazing sensation my body was experiencing.

I felt the most alive I had ever felt in my life. The sun was about an hour before rising, but I could see its rays as we drove down the road. The fragrance of the Spanish moss hanging off the oak trees tantalized my nostrils. The sound of the soft waves pushing against the steps of the lake echoed through my ears, even though we were driving away from it.

I felt like I could run a marathon, and for once in my entire life, my stomach was thoroughly satisfied.

But my heart ached for what I had lost—for what I had done.

Twenty minutes of driving and there was still silence. Finally, Tristen looked over at me before pulling Marilyn into a dim alley and parked.

"Tristen, I—"

"Grace, don't apologize. Please."

He sounded annoyed. I glanced down at my fidgeting fingers. Tristen's hand rested on mine and I peeked over to his direction.

"Don't apologize because this isn't your fault. It's no one's fault." It seemed like he was trying to convince himself of what he was saying.

"What do you mean it's not my fault? Two people are dead right now. One of them...she was...and you killed someone, Tristen. How can this not be my fault?" I asked, hopelessly praying that he would have the answer.

"Grace, this isn't your fault because you have no control over what's happening to you. Do you seriously think that if everything was okay, you would just kill your best friend? And then eat her?"

I shook my head.

"And I didn't mean to kill Eric. I was just trying to get him off of you. There's something wrong with you, Grace. We need to find out what it is. Why do you have this desire to eat people? Do you know anything? Can you think of any reason why you could be doing this?"

"I...I don't know. I mean, I haven't been feeling myself for a little while now. When I ate that cat, I was scared out of my mind and I didn't understand why I did it," I explained. I tried to think all of the events that took place before last night. But everything was a blur.

Tristen must have read the hesitation in my face because he lifted his hand and caressed my cheek in an attempt to soothe me.

"Grace, take your time and think about it. Is there anything we can do? Is there anyone we can talk to who may be able to help us?"

I rattled my brain, determined not to let Tristen down. So much had happened over the last twenty-four hours and it was hard to think of anything else.

"There's a doctor. My mother's friend. He...he wants me to go to an island, and he said he can cure me."

"Well, who is he? Can we call him? When's your mom getting home?" Tristen seemed anxious.

I suddenly felt a strong urge to hear my mother's voice. I searched for my cellphone in my purse. It was early Sunday morning and she was due back late that night. I needed to speak with her. She knew all the answers.

She answered the phone sleepily. "Hello?"

"Mom."

"Grace? What's wrong?" she asked, panic filling her voice.

"Mom, I need you here. Now. Please."

"I'm coming, Gracie." I could hear rummaging in the background. "I'm on my way."

I set the phone down on my lap and took a deep breath. I realized that in just a few hours, Mom would be home and I would finally get the answers I had actually been dreading over the past few weeks. The truth was going to come out, but I wasn't sure it was going to be what I wanted to hear.

I glanced at Tristen, who was waiting patiently for me to say something. "We have to get home. My mom's on her way to the airport now."

"I'm not sure it's safe yet, Grace. I mean, I'm sure they won't find Phoebe and Eric right this second, but the cops may be waiting for you outside of your house because of Sonny."

"We can sneak in. We just have to get home, Tristen. We have to."

And with that, Tristen started the engine.

It only took a few minutes to reach the vicinity of my house. Taking a quick surveillance from the street before mine, there did not seem to be anyone waiting out front. We parked Marilyn and walked cautiously through the neighbor's backyard. A familiarity set in when a memory of Phoebe and me sneaking out of my house one late night to buy junk food at the twenty-four-hour corner store flooded my head. I took a deep breath to avoid any tears.

Once inside my house, I felt the urge to go straight to the refrigerator. But I realized that it was only out of constant repetition and not because I was hungry.

As a matter of fact, I wasn't hungry at all. My stomach still felt completely pleased with what I fed it earlier.

But that thought deeply saddened me.

Tristen must have recognized the expression on my face as we entered the living room. "Grace, are you okay?"

I plopped down on the couch, feeling the weight of everything that happened bearing down on me.

"Yeah, I'm fine," I answered.

Tristen sat beside me. "Grace, it's okay if you're not."

"Are you?"

He sat back into the couch, inhaling deeply. I suddenly felt sadness for Tristen. I wasn't the only one having to endure what happened in the last few hours. He just killed someone to save my life, for God's sake. Was it worth it?

"I'm fine. I guess."

"Tristen, I'm sorry. I know—"

Tristen turned to me, grabbing my face with both his hands and forcing me to look into his amazing eyes.

"Grace, I'm only going to say this one last time. Don't be sorry. Yes, I killed someone. But I was protecting you. It was an instinct. Do you understand?"

I simply nodded.

"I'm freaking out, but I'm not going to yell about it. I don't want to go to jail. We've just got to figure out what we're going to do next. There has to be someone who can help us. I'm in this now, no matter what. Are you okay with that?"

I nodded again.

"Okay," he said before landing a soft kiss on my forehead. "Now, tell me more about this doctor guy."

"Well, he came here a couple of times. The first time, he was visiting with my mom and asked me some questions about how I was feeling and if I was tired, which I thought was really weird. Then, I think I overheard my mom on the phone with him one night. She was telling him that she couldn't send me away. That was all I could hear. And finally, the last time, he was here one morning and offered to take me to some island off the coast of Costa Rica. He said there's a facility there where I can get the treatment I need."

"Did he say what the treatment was for?" Tristen asked. He was concentrating hard on everything I had just revealed.

"No, Phoebe..." I paused.

Tristen touched my knee. "It's okay."

I took a deep breath and fought all the urges to run upstairs and lock myself in my bedroom.

"Phoebe came over and we had to go to school before he could tell me," I finished.

"Well, hopefully when your mom gets home, she can answer those questions for us. In the meantime, maybe we should sleep for a couple of hours. How are you feeling? Stomach-wise, I mean?" he asked, resting a hand on his belly.

"I feel amazing. I'm actually full for the first time in my life," I answered, feeling ashamed for my honesty. After all, I was full of my best friend.

"Okay, why don't we take a shower and come back down here to rest for a bit. I have a feeling today is going to be a long day, too."

Blood rushed to the pores of my face.

"Um...okay. My bathroom is kind of small for the both of us."

Tristen smiled softly and brushed a loose curl from my face. "After everything we have been through, you're still so adorable. I meant we can take a shower separately. I don't think we're ready for a shower together. Do you?"

Kill. Me. Now.

"No! I was...trying to lighten the mood. You can use my mom's shower." I faked a laugh and secretly wished I would crawl out of myself. "I'll give you something to wear. I think my mom kept some of my dad's clothes, maybe a T-shirt and sweatpants."

We headed upstairs and went our separate ways. When I entered my bathroom, I completely avoided the mirror. I knew what would be staring back at me. It would be an image of myself covered in dried blood. Phoebe's blood. And I'd be staring back at a murderer.

After the shower, I dried off and threw on a pair of jeans and a T-shirt. Watching my best friend's blood slide off of my body and into the shower drain took a lot out of me, emotionally. I cried softly, hoping Tristen wouldn't hear. He was already having to deal with enough. Falling apart was something that I needed to hold off on doing in front of him. At least until we knew what we were going to do.

I met Tristen downstairs and grabbed a quilt from the linen closet. Tristen stretched out on the couch, scooting against the back rest to allow room for me to lie down next to him.

As if I had been doing it for years, I nestled into his arms. We spooned, and Tristen wrapped his arms around me, kissing the back of my head as he got settled.

I didn't feel very tired. My body felt awake and alive and almost even shaky with energy. But I could tell that Tristen was exhausted, both physically and mentally.

I wanted to apologize again but remembered that he didn't want me to anymore. Instead, I pushed my body into his and held his arm close.

"Hey," he whispered into my ear.

"Yeah?"

"Everything's going to be okay."

I didn't say anything. I honestly didn't know how to feel. I had just killed my best friend, but her flesh filled my stomach in a way that it had never been filled before. And that somehow overpowered everything else.

THE DEATH

"GRACE ELIZABETH SHELLEY! WAKE up right now!"

I opened my eyes. Tristen sat up instantly, nearly pushing me off the couch.

"What time is it?" I asked, still feeling groggy. I hadn't gone to sleep right away. I had listened to Tristen breath heavily while he slept for a long while before finally dozing off myself. I felt like I had only just fallen asleep.

"It's time for you to tell me what the hell is going on! Why are you sleeping with him on my couch?" Oh, she was pissed.

"Mom, it's not like that. We had a long night. You don't have to yell."

"I'm going to make some lunch," she stated angrily and headed toward the kitchen.

"Seriously? Mom, I'm not hungry."

She turned around quickly, stunned. "What? Grace, what happened?"

Tristen and I glanced at each other. This was it. This was the moment of truth, for both me and my mom. I wasn't sure what I was more afraid of: telling my mother that her daughter was a murderer or finding out what I truly am.

Mom sat down on the loveseat, not breaking her stare into my eyes. I knew she was bracing herself for the worst, and she was going to get it.

"Mom, I...I need to know what is wrong with me." Okay, so I chickened out. Just for now, though.

"Grace, it's very complicated."

"Mom. I need to know. Whatever it is, it's ruining my life. Complicated or not, I need to know and understand what's making my body change and do these crazy things."

"What crazy things?" she asked suspiciously.

Tristen and I glanced at each other again before I answered. "Something terrible happened last night. Something...something that I don't understand." My heart grew heavy.

"Gracie, you're scaring me. What happened?" Her patience was growing thin.

"Ms. Shelley, we need to know why Grace did what she did and what we can do to fix it," Tristen said.

Mom's eyes darted over to Tristen. "Excuse me, but why are you here? This is between my daughter and me. This doesn't concern you."

"As a matter of fact, Mom, he should be here. He killed someone to save my life last night."

My mother's expression morphed into horror. I probably should not have blurted it out the way I did, but Tristen saved my life and he was sticking with me.

I took a deep breath. "Mom, listen to me. Last night was...it was..."

"Tell me, Grace."

Might as well just pull the Band-Aid off. One quick motion. "Sonny and I got into a fight. I bit her arm. Almost all of it. And ate it. Then, we went to Eric's house to hide from the police. In the middle of the night, I...I killed Phoebe and ate her." I swallowed hard and tried not to reminisce on the way her flesh melted into my taste buds. "When Eric woke up, he tried to choke me to death and Tristen hit him with a baseball bat and killed him. Now, we are here."

I cannot recall a time that I had ever seen my mother's expression this way. I guess if I could describe it in one word, I would say: pissedfrightenedworriedperplexedstunned. Yeah, that would sum it up.

"Mom, please tell me. Tell me what's wrong with me and how we can fix it. I'm terrified of what's going to happen next."

Mom looked away, tears pooling at the corners of her eyes. She was hurt most of all, I could tell. I gave her a moment to collect her thoughts. I knew this information was way too much for anyone to handle.

She wiped away a fallen tear from her cheek. "When you were five, you got very sick one day. You couldn't eat a thing. You vomited everything your tiny little body had in it. I figured it could have just been a stomach virus. So, I let another day go by. When you were the same way the next day, I tried to hydrate you myself, giving you medicine and plenty of fluids. On the third day, you were still ill, so I decided to take you to the Children's Hospital. You were in there for a week and no one could figure out what was wrong. You couldn't keep anything down and you were losing pounds by the minute."

She stood up and walked over to the mantel, grabbing an old photo of me.

"I was so disappointed in myself. How could I let my baby girl get so sick? I was a doctor, for God's sake. How could I not figure out what was wrong with my child?"

I remembered the medical file hidden in my mother's closet. The diagnosis: unknown.

Mom placed the picture frame back on the mantel and sat back down on the loveseat. "The doctors tried and tried to get you better, but your little body just wouldn't. It couldn't get better."

I swallowed hard, suddenly getting the aching feeling that this story would only get worse.

"I called Dr. Walker, my colleague. I was a doctor, yes, but child illnesses were not my expertise. It wasn't Mark's specialty either, but I had nowhere else to turn. I needed someone I could trust and confide in regarding your condition."

"Where was Grace's dad?" Tristen asked, completely engrossed in the story.

"Jack was not present at the time. He...he had left me."

"Why?" I asked. Maybe this was my chance to get answers regarding my father, too.

"It's complicated." The heartache that my mother felt for all those years began to show, and I realized then how she must have felt. Alone and scared.

"Mark came the instant I called, but by the time he began his research on your symptoms and reasons for your illness, your condition worsened. You..." She paused to look down at her hands. Tears began streaming down faster.

"Mom, I what?"

"You died, Gracie. For twenty-three minutes. You died."

My heart thudded in my throat. What was she saying?

Tristen wrapped his arm around my body and squeezed me toward him. Did he just hear it, too?

"So...I died?"

My mother was now sobbing. Something I had never seen her do. "Yes. Yes you did, Gracie."

"Well, obviously I'm not dead now. What happened?" My tone was sarcastic, but feelings of betrayal were coursing through me. How could my mother not tell me this piece of vital information before?

"At the time, Mark was in the middle of some developmental research. He had been working on a project for an experimental medication. This medication was being created to help resuscitate patients who just expired."

"So, instead of CPR, this medication would bring you back to life," Tristen stated.

"Exactly. It was an alternative. When injected into the patient, it would revive them. Sort of like what's used when a person is having a severe allergic reaction. Sort of like epinephrine."

"So, he used it on me?"

"I didn't know what else to do. I was desperate to bring you back."

"What was the catch? What were the side effects?" I asked. Surely every medication had a side effect.

"We weren't sure."

"What do you mean?" I asked, becoming increasingly confused.

"Mark had never used it on anyone else. You were his first patient."

"You mean, you didn't know what would happen to me?" I was pissed. How could she not know what it would do to me? It could have turned me into a unicorn for all she and Dr. Walker knew.

"Grace, please don't be upset," she pleaded. "I didn't know what else to do."

Tristen looked over to me. "It worked, Grace. You're alive and here right now."

"I get it." I didn't even want to look at my mother. "Mom, please just tell me when I started to eat animals and humans."

"The night I brought you home, you woke up and...this happened." She lifted her hand in the air to show us the stub of her finger.

"I did that? I thought you had some kind of accident with a fence."

"Yes, you did this. And I was beside myself. I called Mark and explained what happened after I rushed myself to the emergency room. He immediately started some research on why you did it. I continued to keep a watchful eye on things that you did, and you seemed to be okay until about a month later."

"What did I do?" I asked, afraid of what was coming.

"I found you in your closet with the remains of your puppy, Lucy."

I shook my head in disbelief, completely speechless. Tristen hugged me tighter.

"After that, Mark and I worked night and day, trying to figure out what was wrong. You were eating regularly. I fed you normal food, but your body was beginning to deteriorate. You were sluggish. Your hair began to fall out. It was like you were aging a thousand times faster than you should have been."

"Normal food? What does that mean?" I asked.

"Normal food, meaning, what Tristen and I eat."

"I knew it," Tristen mumbled.

I turned toward him. "You knew what?"

"That jerky you gave me last night. It didn't taste like any jerky I'd ever had."

"That's because it's not. It's human meat."

I stood up quickly, no longer able to contain myself. "Wait a minute. Are you telling me that the beef jerky you gave me is from a human? A human person?"

"Yes, Grace. Everything you eat is from a human."

Tristen remained seated, but I began pacing around the living room.

"So, you're saying that everything she eats is from a person. Breakfast, lunch, and dinner?"

"And snacks and juice. Yes."

"Juice? The pomegranate juice? There's human meat in my juice?"

"It's blood and fluids from a human," Mom answered.

How could this be?

"Mom, how can this be? How do you get it? How do you cook it? Tristen and Phoebe have eaten here before."

"I acquire it from work," she stated shamefully. "And the food I give out to your friends is not your food."

"You steal dead people?" I asked. Never in my life would I have ever thought I'd ask a question like that.

"After you had eaten your dog, Lucy, there were some very noticeable changes in your appearance. Your bouncy curls came back. Your coloring was no longer pale. And you were happy and full of energy. Mark started working on a theory. Some research and different tests were performed, and through trial and error, we soon came to realize that human flesh and meat were your source of survival. It was your lifeline."

I sat back down beside Tristen. "So you're saying that the only thing that was keeping me alive was eating humans?"

She ignored my question and continued on with the story. "Mark and I decided that it would be best for us to move out of California and start over. I wasn't going to be able to continue my career with my injury. Mark knew someone at the mortuary here who would hire me."

Megan.

"Do we have family?"

"I have a sister. Megan." Tears formed once again in her eyes. "She has no idea where I am. Where *we* are."

I chose to omit my recent stumble upon Megan's phone number and having actually spoken to her. I was not sure what my mother would think about us communicating.

Mom continued. "I studied different tribes and cultures from all over the world that practice cannibalism. I learned how to cook with human meat and flesh and blood. And once I learned, it became all you ate."

"So...you steal dead bodies from your work?" I asked again, waiting for her to finally answer it. I obviously knew the answer, but I needed to hear it to believe it.

"I take little bits at a time when I'm helping to perform autopsies."

"But, how do you do that without anyone knowing?" Tristen asked.

"I take small amounts then. And when they're being prepped for funerals, I take some from the waist down."

It was making sense to me now. "No one sees that part in the casket," I mumbled under my breath.

Mom didn't respond.

"What's happening to me now? Why am I so hungry all the time? And why do I want to eat actually moving things?"

At that very moment, the doorbell chimed.

Panic washed over me. Tristen and I glanced at each other. They must have found Phoebe and Eric.

THE SERUM

"THAT MUST BE MARK. I phoned him and told him to meet us here," Mom said as she headed toward the front door.

"Wait," Tristen whispered. "You should look out of the window first. It could be the police."

"You two, go hide in the kitchen."

We scurried to the kitchen and waited by the door while mom peeked out the window.

"Are you okay?" Tristen spoke in a low voice into my ear.

"I don't know. I'm just happy I'm finally getting answers."

He swiveled my face toward his. Our lips were inches apart. "Yeah, maybe this doctor can help."

I nodded in agreement and listened closely as my mother opened the front door.

"Oh, thank goodness. Mark, I'm glad you're here."

"Is it bad?"

"Yes."

I grabbed Tristen's hand and headed out to the living room.

Dr. Walker smiled at me. I couldn't quite place it, but there was something off about his demeanor. He strode over in my direction, placing a hand on my shoulder.

"Grace, how are you feeling?"

"I'm feeling confused. Worried. Anxious to know what the hell is wrong with me."

"Grace," Mom scolded.

"It's okay, Veronica."

Another question could be answered. "Wait, is that even your real name?" I asked.

"Let's sit down," Mom insisted.

We all sat in the living room.

"Well?"

"My real name is Eve Romero."

"Romero?"

"Yes," Mom continued. "Your father's last name. My married name. I let you keep your first and middle name. Grace Elizabeth. I changed my entire name because of the exposure I had in my field of medicine. It was part of moving away and starting fresh."

"Dr. Mark. How can you help us?" Tristen asked. His tone was clearly just as anxious as I felt. He was ready to get the bottom of everything. And probably hoping he won't end up in jail.

"Um...and who are you?" Dr. Walker asked.

"He's Tristen. And he stays with me," I answered.

Dr. Walker narrowed his eyes.

"Mark, I was just explaining to Grace everything that has happened up to this point."

"Well, up until why I want to eat cats and humans," I clarified.

"I see. Well, Grace. Your condition is something that we have been studying since the moment we realized what the side effects were." Dr. Walker jumped right into it. "Serum Z was injected into your bloodstream to resuscitate you. The result was supposed to revive you from a lifeless state. It would restore blood circulation and restart your heart. You expired for twenty-three minutes. In most cases, a brain wouldn't last this long without having some kind of brain damage after the subject is revived. If we had brought you back to life through CPR or defibrillation, you would have most likely been brain dead.

"By injecting Serum Z, every function in your body was restored. Your brain was intact, your circulation was restored, and your heart was beating again. However, there were some complications. The serum only worked halfway."

"Halfway?" I asked.

"Serum Z restored only certain parts of your body. And altered others. Your heart still beats. However, your blood is not circulating at its normal potential. Therefore, your heart beats slower than it should. And because your blood circulation is low, it affects everything in your entire body."

"How does eating humans fix that problem?" Tristen asked.

Dr. Walker grabbed the rim of his gold-framed glasses and pulled it closer to his face. "Have you eaten today?"

"It happened," Mom interjected.

"I see."

"Yes, it happened. I killed and ate someone," I murmured.

Dr. Walker inhaled deeply. "Right now, I'm sure you feel completely alive and normal, correct?"

I nodded, almost shamefully.

"When your mother and I discovered the effects that eating human meat and flesh had on your body, we continued to give you what was obviously making you better. Over the years, I have worked day and night to understand why. I am still learning those reasons why, merely because the functions of the human brain and body are mysteries in some cases." He chuckled.

I glared at him. Not funny.

He cleared his throat. "Anyway, simply put, your body is trying to replace what it needs. It is constantly looking for something to allow it to work at its highest potential. The human flesh is replacing what you don't have."

"But, why am I wanting it more and more?"

"When was the last time you have eaten?" he asked. I hesitated, knowing that if I answered that question out loud, I would be choking it out. Tristen sensed my hesitation and answered for me. "It was about four this morning."

"Since I'm assuming this was a very big meal, it pretty much quenched your thirst, so to speak."

I wanted to punch Dr. Walker right in his throat. "Yes, it was a lot," I murmured.

"And you feel better than ever, right?"

I nodded.

"The food your mother was giving you is no longer suitable for your needs. What she was feeding you was that of a deceased person. People who have been dead for some time. They weren't properly stored. Frozen immediately after death. Your mother did a fantastic job, don't get me wrong, but you're beginning to require fresher nourishment. And as you get older, so will your body. What happens when people get older and older? Eventually, they expire. Because Serum Z did not completely restore you, your body has been deteriorating. And at a faster rate than it would normally. You need to eat more often and fresher food to remain in a living state."

"I'm sorry, what?" I asked, leaning in closer as if I hadn't heard what Dr. Walker said. "A living state? You mean, if I don't eat, I will die."

Dr. Walker and my mother glanced in each other's direction, making it completely evident that what I was going to hear next was the icing on the cake.

My mother decided to answer. "Gracie, if you don't get what you need in your body, you..." She paused. I could see her throat gliding up and down, which was an indication to me that she was stifling back tears.

Dr. Walker finished. "One of the major focuses of my research on Serum Z is its ability to grant a subject with immortality."

My jaw dropped as I furiously fought with my brain to ask what the hell he meant. But I couldn't find the words.

"But, how do you know that if you've only been working on it for a little over a decade?" Tristen asked.

"The third subject to be injected with the serum was one hundred and two. She expired due to a heart attack. She is now one hundred and fourteen. As long as she gets the right nourishment, her body shows no signs of deterioration," Dr. Walker explained. "She remains in a living state."

"But what if I don't get the right nourishment? I die, right?"

"I have explored this, and no. You won't die. But your body will remain in a dead state."

"A dead state? You mean, I'm going to walk around...like a zombie?"

"Essentially, yes. You won't have any brain functions, except that of the desire to replace what you have lost."

"How is that possible?" Tristen asked. I assumed he, too, was just as horrified as I was.

Dr. Walker chuckled. "Well, son, that seems to be the million-dollar question."

"A zombie. I'm a real-life zombie," I mumbled.

THE GOODBYE

"GRACE, YOU'RE NOT A zombie. There's no such thing as a zombie." Mom scoffed.

I stared off into space, internally picking up all of my puzzle pieces and placing them together. A large amount of information had been thrown at me in the past forty-five minutes. And even though I finally got the questions I wanted answered and I finally knew what was wrong with me, all I could think about was that...I was a zombie.

My whole life, I had been infatuated with horror movies. I watched the classics like *Halloween* and *Friday the 13th* and realized that sure, those movies could certainly come true because the villain was simply a man wearing a mask, running around brutally murdering people with a knife. Serial killers were real. John Wayne Gacy and Ted Bundy. Real serial killers.

And then I watched horror movies about ghosts and witches and zombies. People believed in ghosts. Some people even practiced witchcraft. But zombies weren't real. People didn't reanimate when they died. It just wasn't real.

Was I the first? Is this the beginning of an apocalypse? A time in history that people a hundred years from now would remember when the undead roamed the streets, killing and eating everything in their sight?

Maybe I was getting a little ahead of myself.

"Grace?"

I turned toward Tristen, who was waiting patiently for me to answer. Then Sonny came to mind.

"Oh my God! Sonny! I bit her! Will she become...like me?" I asked Dr. Walker in a panic.

"No. Grace, this is not some movie. If you bite someone, they won't turn into you. Your condition is only caused by Serum Z. It has to be injected into a subject in order for it to alter anything."

"But I pretty much am a zombie. At least, part zombie."

"Well, we do not refer to our subjects as such," Dr. Walker stated.

"What does the Z in Serum Z stand for then?" Tristen asked.

"Mark, you don't have to talk about this," Mom interrupted.

"No, it's okay, Eve." He removed his glasses and rubbed an eye with his finger before continuing. "Z stands for my son, Zack. He died a few years prior to when your initial illness occurred. CPR and defibrillation were performed on him, but he didn't make it. And that was when I began my search for a more efficient way of reviving someone."

"What did he die of?" I asked.

"Grace, that is something Mark doesn't want to talk about."

"He drowned," he answered.

Silence filled the room.

"Why don't I remember dying?"

"You were a child, honey. You had only just turned five years old. Most people don't remember things at such a young age."

"And the trauma that your body and mind had been through affected your memory," Dr. Walker added.

"You should probably get going soon. Mark, are they waiting outside?" my mother asked, standing up from the loveseat.

I glanced at her. "Is who waiting outside?"

"When your mother called me, I assumed that it was going to be bad news. I know that I asked you if you were willing to come to the island. However, because of the situation and the consequences that have occurred due to your condition, I believe it would be best if you do come."

"So you're going to take me against my will?" I asked, surprised.

Dr. Walker turned to my mother, as if waiting for her to answer the question.

"Gracie, this is only for the best," she said.

"What about Sonny, and Eric and Phoebe?" Tristen asked.

"I'll have my team take care of those things. It shouldn't be anything you have to worry about."

"Nothing we have to worry about?" I asked, raising my tone. Was this guy for real? "I mean, someone is injured and two people are dead. How can I just run away from all of this without anyone finding out it was me?"

Dr. Walker leaned down to my level and rested his hand on my shoulder. "Grace, I have a very intelligent and powerful team of doctors, professors, agents, and government personnel. They're already taking care of things as we speak. Now, the island is going to provide you with everything you need, in addition to the medical attention that you will soon need because it has been a few hours since your last meal. You need to trust me. Can you do that?"

I stared into his steely blue eyes, searching desperately for some sort of sincerity. Some sort of comfort. But there was something about Dr. Mark Walker, something that I couldn't quite place. It felt cold and empty. It felt fake.

I looked over to Tristen. "What about Tristen?"

"Unfortunately, he won't be able to accompany you. I'm going to be honest with you, Grace. When we first arrive on the island, there will be lots of tests to perform. Nothing that you'll have to worry about, but we will need your full attention. It's why your mother isn't coming with us, either. This is only so that we can treat you effectively. But you will be able to communicate with him via video chat and other ways. We have excellent Internet."

I shook my head. "No, that isn't going to work. He needs to come with me." My eyes stayed on Tristen's, and I felt his hand find mine. He smiled, and I knew it was what he wanted, too.

"I'll tell you what, as soon as you are done with testing and settle in, we will arrange transportation and have Tristen come visit."

I turned back to Dr. Walker, searching his eyes for some truth. But I found nothing.

I scanned over to my mother, who was silently crying. I wished I knew what she was feeling. I knew she didn't want her daughter to go, but I also knew that this was out of her hands now. She did what she could, and unfortunately, it was getting out of control. Her daughter murdered someone. What would any mother do?

But to be very honest, I had never been more pissed off at her. She lied to me all these years. About everything. A part of me wanted to understand and I felt like I eventually could, but my anger and disappointment in her was too overwhelming.

I took a deep breath. "Okay. I will go."

Dr. Walker smiled and stood up. "Great! I have to make a call and let my team know we are on our way. Eve, will you please accompany me outside so that we can discuss when you will come visit and what will happen next?"

Dr. Walker calling my mother by her true name sounded really weird.

She nodded. She looked so defeated.

"Mom, I'm just gonna go pack some things. Tristen can come help."

"Okay, dear. I'll be outside."

As Dr. Walker and Mom headed out to the porch, I grabbed Tristen's hand and led him upstairs to my bedroom. Once inside, I closed the door. Tristen walked slowly to my bed, clearly not too happy about my decision.

"Do you need help packing?"

I reached my window and pulled the blinds up. After opening it, I glanced around my backyard.

"What are you doing?" Tristen asked.

"We're getting out of here."

"What? Grace, you're leaving with Dr. Walker. We have to get you packed."

I turned around. "No, we are leaving," I said, gesturing the two of us with my fingers. "I'll pack a small bag with some essentials. I have some of my dad's old T-shirts and sweatpants I can pack for you."

Tristen stood up, complete confusion on his face. "Grace, do you think this is a good idea? Where will we go?"

"Anywhere but that damn island," I answered, pulling some clothes out of my dresser and stuffing them into my backpack.

Tristen grabbed my shoulder, prompting me to stop what I was doing and turn toward him. He obviously had some reservations about this. Did he even want to go with me? Was I jumping the gun with his feelings for me?

He took a deep breath and grabbed my hand. "Grace, as much as I don't want you to go through this alone, I think it might be for the best. Dr. Walker and his team can help you."

I shook my head, protesting what he was saying. "No, something is off about him. I don't trust what he's saying, Tristen. Something's just not right."

"Are you afraid?"

I looked up at him.

"Of course," I mumbled. "Wouldn't you be?"

He smiled. "Yeah, I would. Especially if I was alone."

His thumb grazed my cheekbone, all the way down to my lips. His head tilted to one side, and his eyes softened. I closed my eyes, taking in every feeling his touch left behind on my skin. I braced myself for what was coming next.

I felt in my heart that this was going to be his goodbye. He was going to tell me that I had to go, and that he would make sure to keep in contact with me. That he would write me and video chat with me all the time. That he would come visit me when he could. That he would wait for me. That he would wait for me to come back home.

But he wouldn't.

A tear escaped, leaving behind a cold trail on my cheek. His warm thumb wiped it dry, and I looked up at him again.

"Grace, this isn't goodbye. You know that, right?"

I nodded, but I didn't know that for sure.

"If you stay, I won't be able to help you get better. Sure, I could watch over you and make sure you eat as much as you needed to, but what if you got worse?"

"You mean, what if I eat you," I said.

"Well, you had a chance to. But you didn't. Hey, am I not good enough for you?" he asked playfully.

I contemplated on that for a moment. Why didn't I go for Tristen last night? He was sleeping right next to me.

I smiled back.

"Listen to me. You have to go get better before something else happens. We both know how out of control this can get. We've seen it. But Grace, ever since I saw you sophomore year, I wanted to get to know you. I wanted to be with you. And as insane as all this has been, I still want to be with you. I could fall hard for you. And you have to know how much I don't want you to go. But I'll be here. And when they allow me to go visit you, I'll be there."

"But we can be together now. You're right, I haven't eaten you. Or tried to. We can find a cabin in the woods and live there, and you can hunt for me and everything will be fine. Tristen, I need you. I can't do this alone," I admitted.

Tristen's lips leaned into mine. His hands found my face and I wrapped my arms around his neck. I tried to hold back my tears, but they came anyway as the realization that this might be the last time I would kiss him set in.

I pulled away and continued to fight back the tears that came streaming down my face.

"Grace, you need to do this. I know you can. You'll be okay. And I'll be here waiting for you."

I stared into his eyes, analyzing him just as I did Dr. Walker, trying to find some truth in what he was saying to me.

The fact was this: we hadn't been together long.

Hell, I didn't even know what we were at the moment. But I was leaving to some place far away. And he would be here. He would continue to go to school. Then one day, he'd decide to go visit Sonny to see how she was doing. And then it would happen. They would be together once again, just as they have always found each other after a breakup. And I would be forgotten, or at the very least, remembered as the Creepy Zombie Girl that could have killed him but instead killed someone else and forced him to murder someone, too. He would move on because that was what he probably should have done.

"Grace?"

"I have to finish packing," I said. I carefully let go of him and turned toward my dresser. He didn't say another word.

After painful silences and more packing, we headed back downstairs. Mom and Dr. Walker stood up from the couch and walked over to the door. My mother wiped her eyes with a tissue.

"Are you ready to go, Grace?" Dr. Walker asked.

I ignored him and walked straight over to my mother. I wrapped my arms around her and buried my face into her neck. I didn't fight back my tears. I wanted her to know that I still loved her. But instead of telling her that, I pulled away and whispered into her ear, "I'll never forgive you. I thought that we were in this together. But I guess I was wrong."

She assessed my face.

I could tell she was distraught and not expecting what I had just said. I didn't even expect myself to say it. But it was how I felt. And she needed to know just how much she had hurt me.

I backed away from her, giving her one last look. She was holding her breath and continued to watch my every move as I walked away from her.

Mom stayed on the porch, wiping away her tears as Dr. Walker walked over to the black SUV that was parked in the street. A tall man dressed in a black suit stood stiffly with his hands crossed in front of his groin. Very secret agent-like.

I stopped on the sidewalk and turned toward Tristen.

"Tristen. I just want to say...thank you. Thank you for not running away. Thank you for sticking this out with me. Thank you for...killing someone to save my life." I felt ridiculous for saying that last part, but he had to know that I appreciated what he did.

"Grace, you don't have to thank me."

"No, I do. And I have to apologize. I'm sorry that this will probably be a bad memory for you. I'm sorry that you had to do what you did for me."

"Grace, I did what I had to do to protect you. I'm not sorry for that. And you won't be a bad memory."

I cut him off. "I want you to know that I'll never forget you. I will always remember what you did for me. But we can't do this. I can't put you through this. And I won't make you wait for me."

"Grace, what are saying?" he asked, gripping my hand in his.

I let go, suddenly losing the desire to touch his skin. I didn't want to anymore. It was too painful.

I turned around and took a step toward the car. I felt like a coward, but what else was I supposed to do? I had to end it because I didn't know what was going to happen. And I just couldn't drag him through this crazy situation with me—make him leave school and all his friends to be with some freak.

I had to let him go because I had no idea what my future was going to be like the second I got into that SUV.

The tall Secret Agent Man opened the back door for me, and before I could step into the SUV, Tristen grabbed my arm. I turned around.

"Grace, it's not over."

"Tristen, please," I whispered and pulled away. "I have to go."

"I won't let you go, Shelley. I need more time with you. It isn't over."

I gave him one last look and stepped into the car. The windows were tinted, and I knew he couldn't see me.

I glanced over at my mother, who was now in the frame of the front door. And then to Tristen, who stood motionless on the sidewalk, staring at the tinted window. I closed my eyes, allowing all the tears I held back for him to finally fall.

Secret Agent Man stepped into the driver's seat and Dr. Walker motioned for him to begin driving.

We pulled away, and I looked back one more time.

Was I making the right decision? I wasn't leaving much, but it was my life.

My best friend, who was now dead because of me. Were they going to bury her properly? What about her family?

My mother, who worked my entire life to keep my disease a secret and did unimaginable things to keep me alive. Could I ever forgive her for lying and keeping it all from me?

And Tristen, who murdered someone for me. Whom I still barely even knew but told me he already knew that he could fall in love with me. Even after he found out who I really was. I've liked him for so long. Would I ever get over him?

"Grace, we have a jet waiting for us at the airport. You must be getting hungry. We will have food there for you."

As if on cue, a familiar pain shot through my torso. I didn't look up at him.

There was a moment of silence, then Dr. Walker turned toward me. "Grace, I know you are scared. But you made the right choice. We will take good care of you."

I didn't answer, and he turned back around.

I stared at my hands on my lap, suddenly feeling a sense of loss and emptiness wash over me. I had no idea what was going to happen on that island, but I knew I had to get through it. Alone.

ACKNOWLEDGEMENTS

To my husband, who never stopped believing in me after all these years. Thank you.

ABOUT THE AUTHOR

J.Q. Davis is from New Orleans, Louisiana. She has a bachelor's degree in healthcare but chooses to pursue her dreams of being a writer. Her husband is a retired Marine (23 years!) who works with surgical robots. They don't have kids, but they love to spoil their pups as if they were real little girls.

Her other interests include exercising, listening to indie music, watching anything even remotely related to horror, and reading young adult novels. She is also a video gamer and secretly dreams about being a professional ice skater, volcanologist, and a stop-motion animator.

She is excited to continue this journey through writing and hopes that her readers enjoy her books.

Don't be shy. Leave a review!

Follow J.Q. Davis on:
Twitter: @JoJoQD (https://twitter.com/JoJoQD)
Instagram: @authorj.q.davis
Website: www.jqdavis.com

www.ingramcontent.com/pod-product-compliance
Lightning Source LLC
Chambersburg PA
CBHW061323200626
46813CB00017B/2823

9 781733 337915